Points Club Anthology #1
(The first 6 stories in the Points Club series)

By Marc Stevens

Also by Marc Stevens

Points Club Series

Alan's Gambit
Whipped Cream and Other Delights
Wicked Innocence
Poolside Tryst
Sex and lasers
Raider of the Lost Blonde
Oiled
Points Club Anthology #1

Other Books

That Girl Across the Hall (A Points Club Prequel)
Suburban Spies

First Edition

Lake Scrawls
PUBLISHING

Cover Design: Laurie Mitchell

Contents

Alan's Gambit

By Marc Stevens

Chapter 1

Rumor had it Alan Johnson was hung like a horse. The women whispered and giggled, and the guys just refused to believe. But Tina Atkins knew the rumor was true. She still remembered the night she'd unwrapped that enormous piece of man-meat. How did a guy get that big? He had to be on pills or steroids or something. *God!* The way he'd filled her, she swore he was tickling her tonsils from below. Johnson's Johnson was no myth.

Alan was sharing a drink with some friends on the other side of the Northern Point Supper Club main room. It was still a few minutes until 6:00PM, when the back rooms would open. Of course, a few of the patrons didn't know anything about the back rooms. That was by design. Only the members of the Points Club had access beyond the innocuous door at the back of the barroom.

The North Point Supper Club looked dark and rundown from the outside and few people who didn't know what went on inside even dared to venture through the paint-flecked front doors. The food was unexceptional, the dining room was dingy, and the wait staff indifferent. Harvey Hendricks, the club's owner and bartender, knew who was in Points Club and who wasn't. If you wanted a good drink, one that wasn't watered down, you needed to be in the club.

Harvey slipped from behind the bar into the back room. It was time for his wardrobe change. Cowboy boots, assless chaps, and nothing else. He would have a boner all night and love it.

At the bar, Harvey was replaced by Maya. The pretty woman was a study in goth. Heavily tattooed, lots of black leather and piercings. She had a tendency to send customers who weren't in the club fleeing out the front door with just a growl. Few but club members knew that inside she was a pussycat, and a ton of fun.

Tina checked her phone app for the latest postings for tonight. She really needed points, but she wanted something good—something fun.

Most everyone in the club that was here would be on their phones about now, some posting for partners, some picking up postings that weren't directed at a selected person or persons.

Lots of members wanted something special but didn't care who provided the service. Tina liked to at least have an idea of who she'd be fucking before she picked up the ticket. She was sometimes surprised, but lately had gotten a good idea of who posted for what.

Tina scanned the listings. There were some of the usuals, just wanting a sex partner for straight sex, but there were also usually a few exotic listings, often posted by a mystery person and described in broader terms.

A person could always back out of a scenario, but sometimes it was exciting to take on something adventurous.

So, what do we have available tonight?

She scanned down the list.

Female for Male. 8:30PM. Room 7. Naked. Be ready for anything. 15 points. Spotter needed 5 points.

The fifteen points was a generous offer. But room 7? That was the BSDM dungeon. She avoided that room like the plague. She'd told herself a hundred times she wasn't that kind of girl. Still, every time someone posted, she couldn't help wondering what really went on in there. She wasn't into the whips and chains BSDM stuff, even if she found herself a bit curious about it at times. Was it all pain and torture? That sure as hell wasn't a kink she even wanted to explore.

Give me a hot tub or a soft bed please. And a man with good hands and a big cock.

A man like Alan Johnson.

Yeah, what she really wanted tonight was just an old-fashioned, good fuck with a hot guy. She forced herself to move on.

Female or Male for Male. 8:15PM. Room 1. Oral only. 2 points.

Tina considered snatching that one. It was only 2 points, but a blow job would only take about fifteen minutes, so if there was something later, she could score a little extra. Then her eyes landed on the next offering.

Female for Male (Possibly multiple Males) 8:00PM. Oral & Vaginal. Room 3. Black bra and panties (provided). 7 points (each)

"Holy shit." Her fingers couldn't press accept fast enough. Seriously, seven points for room 3 with possible multiples. Hell, this was her lucky night. Would it be two guys at once, or one right after the other? It didn't matter. She was in.

She scanned the rest of the board, but nothing even came close.

As the clock chimed 6:00, people started jockeying for the back door. There were a couple of non-members dining here tonight, so they needed to use discretion when accessing the back room.

The rule was to allow a little time between, so there was no storming the door. That would attract too much attention, and attention was the last thing

Points Club needed. There seemed to be non-club members in the place a couple of times a week, though God only knew why.

Sliding her card through the reader, Tina felt the door lock give way. She gave the barroom one last glance as she let herself in. Candy Kane shot her a fake frown before she smiled and winked. Mike Meyers raised an eyebrow at her and pointed to his chest. He must have posted something tonight. She hadn't done anything with Mike in a while, but the man's tastes ran a bit too kinky for her anyway. Mike tended to post anonymously. Hopefully, the posting she'd selected wasn't his. Still, he was a nice enough guy, and had a good body, so it wouldn't be the worst thing.

In the back club room, Harvey stood behind the bar. His delicious, washboard abs just visible above the surface. She guessed he was already hard below. She strolled to the bar and glanced down.

Yup. Hard as a rock.

And he'd probably be that way all night. *Well, everyone has their own kink, I guess.*

Harvey was an exhibitionist and bartending at Points Club was the way he satisfied his kinky needs. He smiled and held up a bottle of brandy. "The usual?" He already had a highball glass on the bar with ice cubes.

"That'd be great, Harvey. Thanks." A little alcohol always got her in the mood.

Candy sidled up next to her. "Get something good for tonight?"

The sultry blond was just what her name implied, Candy. Sweet and sexy. The guys, and the girls that swung that way, tended to swing her way whenever they could. And she swung both ways. She was also a favorite in the BSDM dungeon.

"God, Candy, if I told you, you'd hate yourself for not picking it up first. I got lucky tonight."

Candy rolled her hazel eyes. "Then don't tell me. Heck, I'm not even sure I'm playing tonight. Work sucked and I'm bushed. I might just stay here, suck down a few drinks, and pick up whatever falls through the net."

As the night wore on, some of the cheapskates tended to up their anti, and dampen the kink, if it looked like their event wouldn't be picked up. It was a good strategy. Still, Candy pulled out her phone and opened the app. "I suppose I should take a look at what's available though."

Harvey handed her a brandy on the rocks. "Just having you two lovely ladies here has me hard."

Candy laughed. "You're always hard, Harv."

Tina nodded. "God, Harvey, all you do around here, is serve drinks. Don't you ever get laid?" The man was incredibly handsome, ripped and ready for sex.

"That an offer?" There was a twinkle in Harvey's eye.

"Not tonight, stud, but God, man, you gotta get that thing taken care of. You'll burst."

Harvey chuckled, then shifted his gaze to Candy's ample cleavage. "Candy, you want anything?"

"Give me a Harvey Wallbanger...and, no, that wasn't an offer either." Harvey broke into a raucous laugh, as he started mixing her drink.

Tina sipped her brandy and enjoyed the cool burn down the back of her throat.

Jim Burns was the next one through the door. He strolled up to the bar, joining the two women there. He checked his phone. "Damn," he said shaking his head.

Candy laughed out loud. "You're the room seven posting, aren't you?"

Jim shrugged. "Maybe. There's still time to pick it up. I won't tell anyone. You have no idea what you're missing."

Candy snorted. "That's half your problem, Jim. When are you gonna learn how to fill out a request? *Be ready for anything?* Seriously? Even I won't touch that posting."

Jim's smile broadened. "I have my reasons for being vague. You can always stop everything."

Candy shook her head. "I'll spot for you, if you need someone."

"I've gotten multiple requests for spotter already. I think because they all want to know what I'm requesting. Now, if I can just find an adventurous woman."

Tina hugged her phone close. There was no way she was trading her pick tonight, but Candy was right. Jim needed to be more specific, especially with the Points Club shorthand they all used.

Jim leveled his gaze at Tina. "Come on, Tina. I know you've got what it takes. Be brave."

Tina just shook her head. Really, even with the safety of Points Club, the dungeon pushed things further than she knew she could go, especially if she wasn't sure what she'd be dealing with. Jim seemed like a nice enough guy, but he was relatively new to the club. Was any woman willing to take a chance with him in room 7? Well, there were probably a few. Still, that same post had been up the last few weeks, and Tina didn't think it had ever been pulled. And by now, everyone knew it was Jim's.

"I guess I'll just have to see how things go as the night wears on." He sidled up to the bar, and Harvey handed him a long-necked bottle of beer.

Tina shrugged. "Fifteen is a lot of points, and there are some hungry women in the club right now. There was a lot of gifting at the club's annual summer orgy last month."

She was as guilty as the rest, and still kicked herself for getting sucked into that erotic mess. Still, it had been fantastic. She'd gotten off eight times before she'd lost count. Hell, they'd all lost count, and the points had gone right down the drain. Mutual sex with other club members was allowed, but it cost all parties involved. Costs were based on orgasms, and that night there had been lots of orgasms. Tina was down to three measly points, and that didn't buy jack. She sure hoped tonight would pay off. Seven points would put her back in the running. And if she could double that...? Who had that many points to throw around?

Candy was turning on her charms with Jim. "Come on, love. What are you really looking for? Spell it out clearer and you might get lucky tonight." She slid a finger down his chest toward his crotch.

"I'm looking for an adventurous woman." Jim's eyes were devilish. "You up for it?"

Candy grabbed her drink and walked away from the bar. "Not tonight."

Jim took a sip of his beer. "Okay, your loss."

Chapter 2

Alan watched Jim Burns disappear through the door to the back room. He'd seen Tina and Candy, two of the clubs most attractive women, enter before Jim. Could tonight be his lucky night? If his ticket was picked up, he'd be paying big time, but with either of those two it would be well worth it, and if it was Tina...Well, that was a wet dream come true. He counted on Jim Burns running true to form. If he did, there was a chance that Alan could have his fantasy fulfilled tonight and still come out ahead on points.

He patted his companion on the shoulder. "Come on, Bob, it's our turn."

It had taken him months to get his brother, Bob, into Points Club. The screening process was a bitch. Psychiatric tests, physicals, and the approval of two-thirds of the current membership. Points Club members had to be in shape, clean, and mentally stable. This wasn't some backwoods mate swopping group.

But getting Bob into the club was important. Alan was sick of everyone asking him what drugs/exercises/etcetera he did. Okay, he knew he was blessed with an incredibly large cock, but no one believed it was natural. Well, when they saw his brother, they'd have to believe. Hell, the kid had a good half inch on him. Alan would be happy to give up the title of *King Dong*.

He chuckled as he slid his club access card down the slot and opened the door to the back room. His inheritance had made it easy to rack up points, though. As the word spread, lots of women wanted to check out Johnson's Johnson. Well, some of the guys too, but Alan didn't swing that way. He wasn't absolutely sure about his brother's tastes. That could get interesting.

"You know the lingo, right," he said as he ushered his brother toward the bar.

Bob pulled his phone from his pocket. "I think so. But stick around just in case."

Alan patted his brother on the shoulder. "Take a look at what's available and ask me about anything you don't understand." He'd posted his ticket earlier and as he looked over his brother's shoulder at the phone, he noted his event had been picked up by someone. *Nice.* It would be great if it was either Candy or Tina, but really, any of the ladies attending tonight would be fun.

"Okay, what's in room 12 again?"

Alan checked the posting his brother was pointing to.

"Just hand cuffs on the headboard, pretty much the same as room 3. Basically, she wants you handcuffed and naked, so she can have her way with you. She'll want some oral, and there's no guarantee you'll get off at all, but 4 points isn't bad." He chuckled as his brother accepted the event. "Not a bad way to spend your first night in the club."

"Any idea who *she* is?"

Alan laughed. He had his suspicions, and if he was right, bob was in for a treat. "Doesn't really matter, does it? They're all hot or they wouldn't be in the club."

"I guess so. Hey, how many points do you think it would cost me if I wanted—"

Alan cut him off. "Oh no. I've seen the books on your Kindle. I don't even want to know what you're saving for." He gave Bob a shove toward the bar. "Now go...mingle. Get to know people. You gotta make points before you even think about spending 'em."

More people were coming through the door, and Bob started to circulate. Alan didn't worry. Bob was a people person. He'd have no trouble fitting in.

A warm, sexy rumble coursed through Alan and his cock hardened just thinking about what lay ahead this evening. Everything was falling into place. He doublechecked the other posting to make sure it was still available. Of course it was, and he was pretty sure it would be there when he needed it.

He sidled up to the bar, where Harvey already had a whisky sour waiting for him. Tina moved in next to him, so close he could feel the heat of her body, and that was one hot body. God, he hadn't had her for a while, and his cock jumped just at the thought. He should probably offer points outright some night, but he loved playing the game...taking a chance. After all, that's what Points Club was all about.

He'd taken part in some wild and sexy things over the past three years and gotten in over his head once or twice with scenes that took him by surprise. Tonight, it was his chance to turn the tables, and if he'd managed to actually score Tina with his carefully worded ticket...shit, it would be worth every point, even if the bottom fell out of the other half of his gambit.

Chapter 3

The old clock above the bar chimed 7:30, reminding Tina it was time to head to the back rooms to get ready for her event. She wasn't drunk, but had a pleasant buzz tingling through her, that had her ready for some sex.

The black lingerie was already laid out for her in the anteroom. Front clasp bra, yeah, that made sense. It was fun imagining who would be unclasping it.

Someone with a lot of points to blow, no doubt. Well, from the looks of the ticket, she wouldn't be blowing points, but she would be blowing someone. She enjoyed oral sex and salivated at the thought of taking one of the guy's cocks deep in her mouth—drinking down his juices as he came.

She stripped and headed for a shower. Running soapy hands over her body caused a ripple of pleasure to coarse through her. Yeah, she'd had just enough alcohol to get her ready for tonight. She had time, so she lingered under the warm water.

There had been no additional instructions in the anteroom, which made her wonder what kind of fantasy she'd be fulfilling tonight. Stepping out of the shower, she toweled off and slipped into the lacy black panties and bra. She took a deep breath and opened the door to the main room.

She'd been in room 3 many times before. The queen-sized bed was soft, and the sheets always crisp and clean. Points Club went to the max to make their fantasy rooms fun and enjoyable for everyone. The lighting had been dimmed, fresh flowers in vases sent sweet scents wafting through the room, and soft, sultry music floated through the air. Sexy.

Who the hell set this up? What was he expecting? The uncertainty caused her core to flutter. Anticipation always made a night at Points Club so much better.

Then she noted the two sets of furry handcuffs lying on the nightstand. Okay, a little kink. Tina checked that these were the safety handcuffs, the ones with the hidden release. She could never buy into the idea of being really locked in and helpless. That wasn't her style. Just one of the many reasons she avoided room 7. There had never been any incidents. Points Club was scrupulous in its rules. An event in room 7 usually required a spotter—a third Points Club member watching the action in case of any possible danger to either party. Still, that scene wasn't for her. Whips, chains, and pain just wasn't what she was here looking for.

Just give me a nice, straight fuck with a studly guy and no strings attached.

Tina latched the padded cuff around her wrist, then clicked the release, testing it. Yeah, she could do this much kink. With the right guy, she might even enjoy it.

The clock in the room chimed the hour, and she sat on the edge of the bed, waiting. She heard someone in the next room. Her *master* had arrived. Some shuffling, rustling of clothing. He must have been stripping.

Right to business!

Tina had no problem with that.

The door opened slowly to reveal a mountain of tawny skin. Broad shoulders tapered to rippling washboard abs. His bushy black hair shadowed his eyes, giving him a dark demeanor in the dim lighting. He stepped into the room and Tina saw the fire in his eyes.

"Tina." His deep voice reverberated, causing her core to clench. God he was beautiful.

"Alan Johnson." She was instantly on her guard. There were still women in the club willing to pay him points, just to get a look at Johnson's Johnson. Why was he spending his points on a fuck? "Looking for something special tonight?"

His broad smile showed off perfect teeth. "Yeah, you. I was watching when you opened you phone tonight and hoped I'd timed the posting right."

Had he really wanted her? He could have just asked. There had to be something more. Then she remembered the handcuffs on the nightstand. Something ran down her spine, either a thrill or a chill, she couldn't tell which.

"I'm yours to command."

He was wearing just a pair of black boxer-briefs. Inside she could see the huge bulge of his cock straining against the material.

"Then I want you on your knees, in front of me." Tina slid to the floor and his gaze became an evil leer. "That's it. Back straight, keep those perky breasts up."

His crotch was at her eye level now. God that thing was big.

"Stay." He walked behind her. "Now, here's the challenge." She heard him pick up a set of handcuffs. "You have to take down my shorts." He grabbed one hand, pulling it gently behind her, then clasped the handcuff around the wrist. "But you can't use your hands." He pulled back her other hand and cuffed it, before returning to stand in front of her.

His eyes gleamed, catching the firelight of the burning candles. He put his own hands behind his back and just stood there expectantly.

"Isn't this Candy's bit from Marc Steven's new book?"

He chuckled. "Yup, that's where I got it from. It sounded like fun. You up for it?"

Hobbling ahead on her knees, Tina took up the challenge. "The question is: are *you* up *for* it." She knew what he wanted. She moved to his right side and clasped the waistband of his shorts between her teeth, taking it down to mid hip, before it balked.

She scrambled around behind him and bit the back of the waistband. The man's butt was amazing all on its own. Slight dimples on each side greeted her as she tugged down enough to get the elastic band under his rounded gluteal muscles. So firm and tight she was tempted to spring the hidden catch on the cuffs just to get a good grab on them.

She moved around to the other side and pulled once again on the waistband. Of course, there was still resistance on the front. She'd only managed to give his cock more room to grow into. Now came the real challenge.

She hobbled back around to the front. Raising up on her haunches she snagged the waistband among the trimmed pubic hairs at the top of his crotch. His musky, spicy scent filled her nostrils, as she pulled back, riding her nose along the top of his shaft. It seemed endless, and amazingly erotic. She felt moisture seeping from her core. Distracted, for just a moment, she loosened her hold and the waistband slipped from her mouth, snapping back along the top of his cock.

"Good try." Alan chuckled down at her.

She rose up again, determined now, and caught the errant elastic once again, dragging it down and away until Alan's huge cock sprung free, and the boxer-briefs dropped toward the floor.

"Such talent." His rich voice was like silk with just a hint of mischief. "Kiss it."

A drop of precum glistened on the tip, and Tina hungrily brought her lips to it, gently sucking. The salty tang filled her mouth as she twirled her tongue around the head.

"Oh…" He pushed forward.

Tina had trained her gag reaction and prided herself on being able to take guys deep, but there was no way she'd be able to handle this monster. He'd choke her.

Alan must have seen her tense. "Don't worry. I've got other plans for that pretty mouth of yours. Stand up."

Tina stood and Alan made a twirling motion with his hand. She turned her back to him.

Now what?

With a click he removed the handcuffs. "On the bed…facing up…hands over your head."

She scampered to the bed and did as she'd been told. So far, those seven points seemed like a bargain. Alan used both sets of cuffs to attach her wrists to the headboard. "Now the real fun begins."

Once again, she checked for the hidden release, and found it. Tina refused to put herself in the position of being completely out of control in any situation, but with the release available, she could readily lose herself in the fantasy and role-play.

"Let me go, you brute!" She pretended to struggle against the shackles.

"I don't think so." The glint in his eyes was devilish as he sat on the side of the bed next to her. He ran a finger down and around her breast, then slid across the top of the lace that just barely hid her nipple. "Tonight, you're all mine."

"What are you going to do?" She tried to sound scared, but she sure as hell knew what she wanted him to do.

He pulled on the lacy bra, releasing one already-erect nipple. "You want it."

Of course, she did. "No..." She tried to make her voice weak, pitiful, while all the while holding back a chuckle.

Skilled hands released the clasp between her breasts and the firm globes popped free. "Beautiful." His breathing intensified as he cupped and molded her breasts, tweaking the nipples until they were incredibly hard and rosy red.

Molten lava began to move in Tina's core as his lips descended to take one aching bud. He gently sucked and ran his tongue over and around the tight nipple.

"No, stop." She hoped her protest was what he wanted. For seven points he should get his money's worth. Not that points could ever be purchased with money. Sex was the only thing you could barter for points. You had to fulfill someone's fantasy.

And this appeared to be Alan's tonight.

She shivered and ached for more when his lips left her skin. The fire in his eyes intensified. "Now, here's what you're going to do..."

He crawled onto the bed, straddled her stomach, and laid his impressive man-meat right between her breasts. God, it was so big, so long, the tip was poised right above her lips.

"Take it." He pushed his cock toward her mouth. She clamped her lips closed and shook her head.

"Mmm, mmm." His smile told her she was playing it just right.

"Oh, you'll take it alright." His fingers clamped down on her nipple, squeezing hard enough to make her gasp, and sending an erotic shock through her core. As soon as her mouth opened, he slid in. Grasping both breasts he pushed them together, around his shaft, and started to slowly pump. The action brought the tip of his cock almost out of her mouth, then pushed it back in. Tina put her tongue into action.

Okay, maybe a little of the right kind of pain wasn't so bad in the bedroom. Her core was thrumming with delight, and she let a moan rumble in her throat that he couldn't have missed.

"Yeah, Nice. I knew you wanted it."

His heavy sac dragged across her stomach and chest, and his musky man-scent filled the air, as he plunged again and again. His thumbs were working her nipples, and the sensations were unbelievable. She felt herself moisten down below. Oh, she wanted that big cock inside her. But this was his fantasy, not hers.

He was close. She felt his head grow in her mouth, and lashed at it viciously with her tongue, but he suddenly pulled out and away.

"Oh no. I'm not done with you yet."

He scooted down her body, and the head of his cock slid down her neck, between her breasts, and then lower. He pressed his knee between hers, opening her, then knelt between her legs. His fingers played with the waistband of her panties.

"You'll never get away with this." The role-play was only heightening her pleasure.

He pulled, yanking down the lace. "I already have."

God, he made a gorgeous villain. His cock stood out strongly pulsing, as he pulled down her panties, raising her legs to rip the lacy garment from her. She knew he was close. His cock pulsed and moisture seeped from its spongy head. But he took his time, running his eager fingers along her folds, testing her slickness. A woman had to be ready for him, and Tina knew Alan understood that.

But she was so slick, so ready for him. As big as he was, he easily slid into her wet channel. As he plunged to the hilt, she saw his face scrunch. He reached up and released the cuffs.

"God, Tina, when I'm with you, I don't need a fantasy. You are the fucking fantasy."

She smiled and brought her arms around his neck, pulling him toward her and locking her lips on his. He tasted so good. Their tongues tangled as he began to pump that incredible cock into her.

She broke the kiss and grinned. "Told you you'd never get away with it."

Her insides exploded as he intensified his thrusts. Waves of passion swept over her. God, he filled her so completely, his cock touched every part of her core, and it was all tingling as it stretched around his massive girth. She feared she'd have trouble walking after this, but it would be so worth it.

She felt him grow inside her, and he closed his eyes, growling as he thrust one final time to the hilt. Her passion spilled over, rocking her to her core, as he emptied himself into her. Spurt after hot spurt thundered through her, as she shook uncontrollably in his arms.

For long moments she could only hold on to his muscular arms as an orgasm rumbled through her. He collapsed on top of her, his heavy warmth like a blanket of passion.

"God, what you do to me..." He rasped. His breath fluttered hot against her neck.

Tina's heart thundered in her chest. Her head spun in wonder. She'd have paid him points for this feeling; she hoped he'd gotten what he wanted.

"Was that what you were looking for?"

He pulled her close and rolled to the side, bringing her with him. His heavy sigh was filled with desire. "So worth the points."

She snuggled into his embrace and they lay in the warmth for long moments.

Tina hesitated even bringing it up, she was so enjoying the warmth of being in his embrace, but she really needed the points, so she finally broke from his embrace. "Your event mentioned a possible second encounter?"

His chuckle was more a rumble in his throat. "Let's shower and dress. It's in another room. You'll have to decide if you want the points when we get there."

"Not even a hint?" She was intrigued.

"Nope, but if you let me shower with you, I'll scrub your back."

Chapter 4

The feeling in the pit of Alan's stomach was something between a thrill and a chill. How would Tina react? They'd playfully bantered and toyed with each other during their steamy shower together, but now she was quiet. This would be a big gamble, and he knew it.

And a lot of points were riding on Tina's next decision.

He'd seen Tina pull out her phone the moment she'd settled into the outer dining room earlier that evening. He'd used his iPhone to send in the event at just the right moment to hopefully catch her eye. This would have worked with just about any of the women in the club, but Tina made it extra special. He knew how she felt about room 7. She'd avoided it like the plague, and for good reason. Could he talk her into it tonight? The challenge had been more than he could resist.

And she'd bitten. He couldn't wait to see her face if he could get her to step inside the staged event.

She took a step back when he stopped in front of the door. "The ticket didn't say anything about room 7."

This was it. The big gambit. God, but he loved the game. "You can back out at any time. Aren't you at least curious?"

She was shaking her head from side to side. Her eyes were dark when she looked up into his. "I guess I just never though you…"

"You don't even know what's set up in there. Don't you trust me?" Did she? He wanted her to trust him so badly, and not just because of the game he was playing tonight. There was something about Tina.

The thing about Points Club was it let you get to know someone on a completely different level. You got to know their deepest, darkest fantasies. That was something most people rarely found out; even with people they thought they knew pretty well. Sometimes you just endured the role-play to get the points, other times it was easy to throw yourself into someone's fantasy.

He'd always enjoyed being part of Tina's fantasies, and he got the feeling she liked most of his. There was an honesty and trust building between them. Alan wasn't ready to settle down yet. He loved the sexual highs and variety he got from being a part of Points Club. But lately, he'd been thinking a lot about Tina. She was definitely the kind of woman he could settle down with...eventually.

Tina took a step toward the door and lifted her hand toward the knob. She took a deep breath, and Alan watched those wonderful breasts rise and fall. "Okay."

The anteroom was similar to the one they'd just left. A place to dress or undress, shower and address any special instructions. The small sheet of paper on the dressing table had only one word on it: *Naked.*

***

Tina certainly didn't have any problem getting naked in front of Alan. Hell, she'd just been. Their shower together had been invigorating and playful. If she hadn't been so point-poor, she'd have given *him* a few for a round of just straight up sex.

As she stripped out of her clothes for the second time in less than an hour, she had to wonder what was running through Alan's mind, though. Room 7? *Ugh!* There were some things she just didn't want to even try.

The clock in the room struck 8:30. At the same moment something struck Tina as familiar.

25

Clear as the chiming clock she remembered the ticket.

Female for Male. 8:30PM. Room 7. Naked. Be ready for anything. 15 points.

"Didn't Jim Burns have this room reserved for 8:30?" Alan just raised an eyebrow and gave her a quirky half-smile.

Well, she was here and she was naked. She might as well go in. She always had the option to back out.

Room 7 was dimly lit, but there was enough illumination to see the iron maiden in the corner, the pool cue rack lined with whips and torture implements, and the various benches and tables. Chains hung from the walls and ceiling like decoration, but they weren't just embellishments. No expense had been spared to make the room look and feel like a medieval dungeon. A chill ran up Tina's spine. What could Alan possibly want with her here?

Then her eyes widened. In the center of the room, suspended by manacles and long chains attached to the ceiling, hung a man. A blindfold was tied around his eyes, and noise-canceling headphones were over his ears. Still, Tina recognized Jim Burns' solid frame.

"What's going on?"

Jim was hung in a way that only his tiptoes could reach the ground. He was completely naked and semi-hard.

Alan handed her a second sheet of instructions from the table just inside the room.

Do whatever it takes to get me off and the points are yours.

"Seriously?"

Alan chuckled. "There's your next seven points, if you want them."

God, this would be easy. Was this what Jim had wanted all these weeks? He should have been more specific. Women would have lined up for this one.

Tina approached Jim. She knew he couldn't hear or see her. He probably wasn't even aware there was anyone in the room. He jumped a bit when she placed her hand on his butt.

Jim had a nice butt, tanned and well-toned. His muscles rippled as she ran her hand across his firm ass cheeks. She gave him a bit of a whack with the flat of her hand and he gasped, then sighed. His cock rose to full attention.

"Oh Jim, you naughty boy." She chuckled when he didn't respond. He must really have been unable to hear her.

She knelt in front of him, blowing hot breath across his pulsing penis. He was nowhere as large as Alan, but he was still quite ample. Tina tried to remember if she'd ever had Jim before in another scenario. She put the palm of her hand on his broad chest then dragged it down across his rippling abs, but she avoided touching his shaft. Not yet. She'd give him is points' worth.

She shifted and brought her head underneath to run her tongue along the bottom of his sac.

"Ohhh..." Jim quivered at her light touch.

She gently sucked one of his balls into her mouth, running her tongue over and around it. His cock bobbed above, the head turning a dark purple as a bead of fluid seeped from the slit.

Tina never thought about what it would be like to have a man so totally in her power. She released his balls and dragged her tongue along the underside of Jim's cock, then took the head into her mouth. She rolled her tongue around the tip and felt it expand. This wouldn't take long. He had to be right on the edge.

She wrapped one hand around his shaft, and used the other to cup his balls, then began working him with her lips, tongue and teeth. He was panting hard, his muscles all tense. Suddenly he let out a gargling cry and came. Ribbons of hot jism spurted into her mouth, and Tina greedily sucked it all in, swallowing when she could. No reason to mess the place up.

Club members each took turns with cleaning and maintenance duties on the rooms, so they tended to look after things when they could, as long as it didn't interfere with the fantasy. A swallowed load was one less thing to clean up afterward. And Tina didn't mind swallowing.

Jim was still shaking, as his erection started to shrink. His breath came in short gasps. "Awesome!" He was smiling broadly.

Alan cranked down the chains and brought the key over to unlock the manacles. As he pulled off the earphones and blindfold, Jim blinked. "Tina? So, you went back and switch events?"

Alan laughed, waving his phone at Jim. "Not exactly. The jig's up, fancy pants."

Jim just smiled and shook his head. "You son of a bitch."

Tina wasn't sure what was going on. "You guys want to let me in on the joke?"

Alan continued chuckling and looking smug. "Get dressed and meet me in the bar. I'll give you your points then. In the meantime, Jim can fill you in."

Jim came over and gave Tina a hug. "Wow, I never expected anything like that. You are amazing. I just wish I could give you all the points. We both got screwed tonight. That's the last time I trust Alan."

"So, are you going to tell me the specifics?" Now Tina was very curious.

Jim nodded. "Alan sure knows how to play the game, I'll give him that. Go ahead, get dressed. I'll give you some privacy. Then I'll tell you whatever you haven't figured out."

Tina grabbed Jim's hand and pulled him toward the dressing room. "Oh, come on. It's not like I don't know what you look like naked."

As Tina shrugged back into her clothes, curiosity crept up on her. "Jim...your fantasy out there...want to tell me about it?"

She could ask, but he was under no obligation to answer. Fantasies were personal, and this would always stay just between them either way unless Jim decided to share the encounter with Marc Stevens to write up.

Jim shrugged. "Sure." He looked her straight in the eye. No shame. Very secure in his sexuality. Tina respected that.

"Where I work, I have five hundred people under me that I'm personally responsible for to the board of directors. I deal with shit every day. Everyone wants *me* to handle *their* problems. Sometimes I just want to be completely out of control. Let someone else take charge and make decisions. You gave me just what I was looking for...and so much more."

"You could have gotten that for a lot fewer points. Hell, a standard blow job goes for three points lately. Your fantasy wasn't much more than that really. Why weren't you more specific?"

Jim chuckled. "I was doing some betting on the side, placing a few points each night I posted that no one would pick my event. Bets are blind, so no one knew it was me. There are some in the club that will take just about any bet put out there. I got more into the betting than actually having my fantasy fulfilled. I figured no matter what happened, I would win. I racked up thirteen points over the

29

past three weeks just doing nothing, and stood to make another five this week, which would have completely paid for my event if Alan hadn't screwed things up."

Tina had never used the betting part of the Points Club app. She couldn't conceive why people would bet on other people taking or not taking certain events, but she knew lots of the others placed bets all the time on lots of different things. It was just another way to earn (or lose) points.

"So, you were betting against yourself?"

"I've been raising the points on the ticket each week, to up the stakes, and making a killing when no one would pick it. So, either I got my fantasy, or I made points off not getting it. Either way, I got a thrill."

It was quite a scam, and completely legal under the Points Club charter. Jim was a smart guy. "So how did Alan find out?"

Jim shook his head as he slipped back into his jeans. "Last week someone actually pulled the event. I needed a spotter, because it was room 7, so I asked Alan. Whoever it was, never showed. They must have backed out at the last minute, but Alan had seen the whole set up. I had a feeling the jig was up, when he offered to spot for me again tonight, when someone picked the ticket."

"But I didn't pick up your ticket."

"I know," he said. "Alan did, the rat."

Tina finished dressing and headed out to the barroom area. She wanted to get her points from Alan, and she needed a drink.

Chapter 5

Everyone in the barroom had gathered around the bar. Alan was satisfied with the way the night had turned out, but it looked like he'd have to wait a while to get a drink.

"Candy! Candy! Candy!" The crowd chanted lustily.

Harvey was up against the back counter. His face was scrunched up and his eyes were closed as he grasped the countertop edge. Kneeling between his legs, Candy was working her magic. The willowy blond had her face in Harvey's crotch and was bobbing her head like she meant business.

"How long?" Harvey cried out. His teeth were clenched and his body shook. He was hammering the back of his head into the cabinet behind him.

Bill Tomkins was looking at his watch. "Only three and a half minutes, Harvey. You're gonna have to hold on a bit longer."

Candy reached up and gave Harvey's balls a squeeze.

"Shit, no fair." Harvey cried out as his body convulsed. Candy locked her lips around the head of his cock and sucked down his orgasm.

Harvey sighed heavily, as Candy rose with a big smile on her face. An errant dribble headed toward her chin, but she caught it with her finger and guided it back up to her pert lips. Then she held up her arms in victory. "The winner!"

The crowd cheered and Alan looked down to see that Tina had joined him. "Now that's what I call a Harvey Wallbanger."

Candy looked over at Tina's comment. "Damn straight!" She ran a finger down Harvey's bare chest. "That'll teach you to bet against my tongue."

Harvey got busy mixing drinks again and Candy worked her way over to Tina and Alan.

"So how much did you soak Harvey for?" Alan asked.

Candy glowed. "Four points," then she raised her voice, "and a round of drinks for the house!"

Another huge cheer filled the barroom, as Harvey scowled at Candy.

Alan laughed and pulled his smart phone from his pocket. "Time to pay up for your services tonight." He nodded at Tina. "I believe I owe you 14 points."

***

Tina confirmed the point transfer on her own phone. Yes, she was back in the game. She looked over at Alan's display to check his points. She was shocked. "You actually made 4 points tonight?"

Alan held up Jim's 15-point ticket. "I also placed a 3-point bet that the ticket would be pulled tonight."

Jim came up on her other side. "You cost me 18 points, Johnson." He confirmed the transfer on his own phone then threw his arm around Tina's shoulder and planted a kiss on her cheek. "And it was worth every stinkin' point."

Harvey came over and placed a brandy on the rocks in front of Tina. "Everyone have a good night? Any points disputes?"

Tina looked at Alan, then over at Jim. She shook her head. "None here."

Jim's hard body, Alan's incredible cock, and 14 big points, tonight was a good night at Points Club.

Whipped Cream and Other Delights

By Marc Stevens

Chapter 1

Harvey's bright smile greeted Marc, as he entered the North Point Supper Club. It was just after 2:00 PM and the place was empty except for the tall bartender.

"You're a little early," Harvey said. He finished polishing a high-ball glass and set it on the tray behind him. "Club doesn't start until six, you know."

Marc nodded. "Vicky and I cooked up something special last night over dinner, a very fun scene, and I wondered if there was still time to set something up before tonight."

Marc and Vicky had been exploring their *foodiness* and each other on a regular basis lately. It wasn't actually dating…but it was.

He liked her a lot, and they had a shared interest in all things gastronomic. Still, neither of them was looking for anything past that.

Harvey chuckled. "This has got to have something to do with food, if I know you two."

Yeah, he knew them well, and Harvey followed Marc's blog closely.

"I want to try out something a little messy. Do you have any rooms available that can handle that?"

Harvey motioned him back and hit the release button for the back door. Marc scanned his card and opened the door. The big bartender met him in the club room.

"After reading your blog about sexy fruit, I had a feeling you might be in today. Okay, I was hoping you'd be in today, so I was playing around with room five this morning." Harvey's smile was infectious. "I'm really looking forward to reading this story."

"My guess is, it's going to get pretty messy." Marc was heading into erotic territory he'd never imagined just a week ago.

Harvey's laugh filled the hallway. "Like we've never done anything messy back here before."

Marc could only imagine. The Points Club was a unique group of people dedicated to fulfilling each other's sexual fantasies. Every effort was made to make things as realistic as possible. They had everything from dozens of specialized bedrooms and bathrooms, to a fully functioning medieval dungeon. Harvey somehow produced furnishings in amazing variety as needed, and even had access to exotic and specialized outdoor settings.

Marc had recently stumbled his way into the group and found it offered the perfect place to research his writing. So many of the members were eager to tell him about their erotic adventures here. Story ideas were stacking up on his laptop, but this one was something he particularly wanted to pursue for himself. Thank goodness Marc's needs for tonight would probably be simple and straightforward.

The anti-room had a nice, big shower stall, big enough to fit four people comfortably if necessary. There was a rack to hang clothes, comfortable seating, and a nice dressing table. Room five itself was small, containing only a double bed and a couple of occasional chairs.

"Vinyl sheets on the bed, plastic covers for the chairs, and tile on the floors should make cleanup a snap," Harvey said. His eyes grew serious. "And you are responsible for all cleanup."

It was fair enough. It was his fantasy. Though, Vicky had offered to help with the cleanup after.

Marc nodded toward Harvey, who went to a closet and produced a rolling, hospital tray table, the kind that could be suspended over the bed for easy access.

"I figured this would make things a bit more convenient. And here." Harvey placed a new jar of Maraschino cherries on the table then shot Marc a wink. "A little donation to the cause."

Marc couldn't help but smile. Things were coming together nicely. "Harvey, this will be perfect."

Chapter 2

Vicky Majors got wet just thinking about what Marc had planned. *Delicious.* It was the best way to describe the event...and the man who was planning it.

She was Nurse Vicky to just about everyone she knew. As a nurse at Mercy General Hospital, her shifts were varied and sometimes unbearably long. She had very little time for dating and romance. Her one relief, on the nights she did get off, was Points Club. No hassles or hang-ups, and none of the complications of a *relationship.* It was just what she needed—raw, fulfilling sex. Points Club was really just a big group of *friends with benefits*...but there were a lot of benefits.

When Marc Stevens was wheeled into her unit a few weeks ago, she'd thought the man a goner. His vitals were low, and scans showed potential brain damage, yet Marc had recovered overnight. And fully recovered!

When she'd brought him in his breakfast that morning, he'd been alert and talkative.

And hungry.

Not that the hospital food was anything to speak of, but it was there she'd first got in inkling of his foodie obsession...something she shared.

She was surprised to find out he was the writer of some very sexy stories. The Points Club gang had all been buzzing about it, and when she found out Marc was in Points Club, all bets were off.

Sex with Marc had been great, and the dinners out had been an added bonus, but they really hadn't done anything worthy of one of his stories until this.

The five points didn't mean a thing. She was going to be in one of his stories, and that was something most of the club members had been clamoring for.

Oh, he was publishing them as fiction, changing names and such, but the club members all knew the truth. The club's anonymity clause kept everything that went on in the closed rooms of the club a secret, even from the other members, but Marc's membership had opened the doors. Members were signing off, and giving up dark details, just in hopes of getting into one of his stories.

Vicky had already signed off, no matter what happened tonight, and all the Points Club members were jealous of her. She smiled a secret smile. This was going to be juicy, in more ways than one.

Chapter 3

Marc pushed the grocery cart through the store, gathering the items he needed. A can of pineapple rings, fresh strawberries, navel oranges, a couple of bananas, and a large bottle of chocolate syrup already occupied the cart. He weighed the spray bottle of whipped cream and decided to get two. It wouldn't pay to run out.

Then he was off to the alcohol section of the store to pick up a rich, sweet Zinfandel Port from a local winery. It would go great with the fruit and chocolate. Tonight promised to bring a new meaning to the phrase *full bodied*.

His cock was hard and his taste buds tantalized as he turned down the nut aisle. He winced at the idea of *crushed nuts*, but they'd add a needed salty bonus to the mix.

***

Vicky's core seeped and her stomach jumped as she parked her car in the lot outside the North Point Supper Club. This would either be incredibly erotic or a complete disaster. In all her years in the Points Club she'd never tried anything as off-beat as this, but that's what made the club so much fun. You just never knew what someone would come up with to try. At the very least, it should be an interesting experience.

She'd barely stepped through the doorway when it started.

"Well, don't you look good enough to eat," Alan Johnson said.

"I hear Marc has something really sweet planned for you," Tina chimed in.

Vicky smiled but held up her hands. "Stop...just stop." Then her stomach fluttered. "He is here, isn't he?"

Candy chuckled. "He breezed in with two shopping bags full, about fifteen minutes ago. Harvey let him in early to finish setting everything up."

It was just a few minutes before six, when the back room would open for the club members. Vicky wondered if she should order a drink out here or wait to get one from Harvey in the back room. She opted to wait. Harvey's endless antics usually made the experience of ordering a drink into an enjoyable adventure.

She edged toward the back door, anticipation filling her with an excited tingle. She was eager to get in and get at it. Tina made a move toward the door also, but then smiled and shot her a wink. They all could probably tell how anxious she was.

Suddenly she was surrounded by a crowd of people. Looking around she realized that this was one of those rare nights everyone in the place was a club member. As long as no one else walked through the front door in the next two minutes, it would be acceptable to storm the back door.

There looked to be some eager people in the group. It was easy to see there were a few other arrangements made for tonight. The stuff that went down in the back rooms could fill volumes. Now that Marc was in the club...it eventually would.

Everyone wanted to come up with a story that would grab Marc's attention. It was the new *thing* and bets were being placed on the story that Marc would publish next...after the one he'd be writing about her tonight. That was a for-sure unless it turned into a mess.

Who knows, maybe he'd write it up even if it was a disaster.

Harvey was behind the bar, already lining up drinks for the regulars. Dressed in cowboy boots, assless chaps, and nothing else, Harvey was a class

A exhibitionist. His cock stood at attention as he moved fluidly behind the bar. He knew everybody's favorite drink, and usually just kept them coming as long as you stood at the bar. He was already grabbing for a Margarita glass as Vicky approached, but he stopped.

"Considering what Marc is setting up back there, I'm thinking maybe you won't want your usual tonight."

The big bartender had a point. There was probably going to be enough sugar hitting her system in the next few hours. "How about a Gin and Tonic?"

Harvey smiled. "Excellent choice."

Yeah, something light and refreshing to cleanse the palate.

She felt Marc behind her before she heard him. "Hey, Vicky." His voice rumbled with sexy innuendo. He twined his arms around her waist and hugged her from behind, bringing his lips to her ear. She could feel his clean, hard lines as he held her, his erection evident against her ass. He nibbled her ear then whispered, "You ready for tonight?"

God, she was positively dripping.

Chapter 4

Mark loosened his grip and Vicky turned in his arms, planting a searing kiss on his mouth. Soft, firm lips took her away from the noise and commotion of the crowded barroom. Public displays of affection were not only approved here but expected most nights.

When she finally pulled back, she was breathless. "Let's do this."

Marc pulled her out of the club room, and down the hallway toward room five. In the anti-room he started to undress, pulling his T-shirt off over his head. His sculpted chest was a sight to relish, and Vicky did just that.

"I figure this is one time we want to do the *dishes* before and after the meal," he suggested, nodding toward the large shower chamber.

"I'll wash yours if you'll wash mine."

Marc moved behind her and helped her undo her bra. His hands came around and cupped her naked breasts. Vicky felt her nipples pucker under his caress.

"I do like your dishes," he said.

Yeah, it was going to be one of those nights. "Sir, I will need to inspect your serving utensil." She turned in his arms again and undid the button of his jeans then yanked down the zipper.

His cock sprung free, rigid in her hand as she stroked him. Long and thick, she delighted in the velvety smooth shaft.

In a jumble of awkward kisses and caresses they laughed and divested each other of their remaining garments. Marc grabbed a washing puff and a bottle of body wash from the cabinet and dragged her toward the showers. As the hot jets of water turned the room to steam, Marc spilled a generous amount of body wash into the puff and started in on her. She sighed as he worked her back and squealed as he moved lower to her ass and between her legs.

By the time he'd finished her skin was tingling and her body flush with excitement. She held out her hands and he deposited the puff and wash in them. She worked up a good lather and whisked the scrubber and her ready hands over his hard body, lingering and playing with his muscular chest, hard rippling abs, and short, trimmed pubic hairs. He'd been hairier down there when he was in the hospital, and she loved the thought of him manscaping just for her.

She wrapped one slick, soapy hand around his throbbing shaft and brought the puff up from underneath, gently scrubbing his sac, and running it up the underside of his cock.

"Keep that up and you'll have some cream before we even get started." His look was pure devilishness.

They rinsed off and toweled dry, then moved into the bedroom setting. The rolling table held an assortment of items, and as she looked over the fruit, and other goodies, ideas started to flow.

Marc raised an eyebrow at her. "Do you want to go first, or should I?"

She pushed him down onto the bed. "Lay down, buster. I'm about to reinvent the banana split."

Chapter 5

Marc had to hold his breath, and hold back his ejaculation, as Vicky pulled and pushed to get the spongy head of his cock through the hole in the center of the pineapple slice.

"You're just too thick," she said, giving up on her attempt to wiggle the fruit slice down his shaft. She left it, looking like a yellow umbrella shading his balls, as she reached for the can of whipped cream. She spurted the cold fluffy topping around the head and up to completely cover the tip of his cock, then ran another ring of whipped topping around the base of his shaft and over his sac. She grabbed a large strawberry and nestled it in the hollow created between his balls, then placed a Marciano cherry on the very top of the pile of whipped cream on the head of his cock.

Marc had to hold back from laughing and shaking everything apart.

"Just one last touch," she said, reaching for the chocolate syrup. She drizzled his entire package, then sat back licking her lips and admiring her masterpiece. "That's what I call a banana split."

"But there's no banana," Marc argued.

"Oh, there's a banana." She chuckled. "One, very big, very ripe banana."

She bent down to nibble at the pineapple ring, and suck in some of the whipping cream from around the head of his cock then slid her tongue down his shaft, licking down a trail of chocolate syrup that had leaked down his shaft.

"You've never tasted better."

She plucked the strawberry from the base of his shaft, and ran the red fruit through the cream and chocolate mixture pooling in his crotch.

"Kiss me," she said, taking the strawberry in her teeth and moving up toward him on the bed.

Marc opened his jaw and took his half of the berry in, biting down and tasting the sweet juices explode in his mouth and run down his throat as his lips moved across hers. Strawberry, chocolate and whipped cream melded with the taste of the woman herself. Sweet beyond belief he consumed her lips, hastily swallowing the fruit to make room for her tongue in his anxious mouth.

As she kissed him, she ran cool fingers over his chest, tweaking his hardening nipples. Down below his cock grew, causing the bite ridden pineapple to split and the pieces to fall into the puddle of cream at the base of his shaft.

Vicky broke off the kiss. She scanned down his body to the ruins of her *banana split* below. As she moved back down toward it, she grabbed up the can of whipping cream, and squirted a small puff on each of his nipples, then spent some time licking it off.

Her tongue sent a ripple through him each time she flicked it of one of his erect nipples.

Finishing there, she scanned the table of foodstuffs.

"Ohhh! Nuts!"

She palmed a handful of crushed peanuts and sprinkled them over his shaft and balls. Then her tongue went to work. Licking around to outside, and cleaning up everything as she moved inward, she lapped up cream and chocolate, pineapple pieces, and peanuts. She pulled each of his balls individually into her mouth, sucking on them gently, then started up his shaft. Somehow Marc had managed to keep the cherry balanced in the cloud of whipped cream at the top of his shaft, and Vicky's grin was wide as she descended on it, pulling the fruit and the head of his cock into her mouth.

It was more than Marc could stand. As her lips locked around the head, slurping in the last of the whipped cream, he orgasmed, adding his own cream to the mix.

"Sorry," he groaned as Vicky continued to slurp and suck.

Chapter 6

As Marc emptied himself in her mouth, a sensational smorgasbord of taste sensations exploded on Vicky's tongue. Sweet cream, dark chocolate, tangy cherry, and the thick, salty taste that was all man, melded together. *Indescribably delicious* was the phrase that came to mind. She would have thought the combination distasteful, but she found it not only good, but incredibly sexy. Her stomach flipped and her core flamed as she eagerly lapped up every tasty drop.

How would she describe it to Marc? He'd ask her, she knew, for his story. A rich, salted caramel sauce was as close as she could come in comparison, but even that fell far short of the orgasmic taste that filled her. As the last, trickling drop slid down her throat, she threw herself into his arms.

"That was amazing!"

She locked her lips on his and rolled with him on the bed. His tongue tangled with hers, and her head spun as he rolled her over and ended up on top. His semi-hard cock throbbed against her stomach.

He rose and his eyes darkened mischievously. "My turn."

***

How could he even come close to matching what Vicky had just done to him...for him? He'd never thought this challenge would lead to anything near that sexually fulfilling. Now Marc wanted to give her as intense an experience...if he could.

He positioned himself between her legs and ran a tentative finger along her folds. Wet and ready, he started by pealing a banana. Gently he slid the fruit up into her, wiggling it a little as he moved it deeper.

"Oh!"

Whipped cream was next, along each side of her folds filling the creases at the V of her torso. Next, he nestled two navel orange slices in the cream on either side of the banana. The end of the banana sticking out looked disturbingly like a cock, so he broke off the end, leaving only about an inch sticking out of her opening.

Much better.

The crowning touch was a Marciano cherry, positioned in the whipped cream right over her clitoris. Vicky chuckled, threatening to upset the fruit cart, as Marc drizzled chocolate sauce over the whole thing.

"I suppose now you want my cherry," Vicky said.

Chapter 7

Marc was licking his lips as he poised over his creation. The banana filling her, and the cool, melting whipped cream running between her legs was surprisingly arousing. Vicky felt herself seeping, adding her own essence to the puddling mass.

He started low, licking up both sides around the banana, and sucking the orange slices into his mouth.

"You taste amazing." He left a small pillow of cream and the cherry up on top as he locked his lips around the banana. He sucked it into his mouth, then pushed it back into her a couple of times. Finally, bite by bite, he pulled it out of her, consuming it as he went.

Her clit throbbed, begging to be touched, beneath the spray of whipping cream and cherry, but he didn't go there right away. Instead, he reached for the can of whipped cream again. Moving up he covered the tip of first one breast, then the other, in a mound of cream, then buried a small strawberry in each pile. "This is only fair," he said with a leer.

He drizzled more chocolate sauce over each then created a trail of chocolate that led from the valley between her breasts, down toward her belly button. Finally, he popped the cork on the bottle of port wine, and poured a small amount into her navel, filling the cavity.

"Yeah, you do look good enough to eat."

Marc started back between her legs, his tongue sliding up her folds, at last fondling her clit with his tongue, as he sucked the cherry and last of the cream into his mouth. He slid two fingers into her as he continued to trail his tongue over her mons and up toward her belly button. Like a thirsty canine, he lapped up the wine, and began to slide his fingers in and out of her folds.

Vicky tried to stay as still as possible. The whipped cream was starting to melt, and slide down her breasts, and her core was erupting under Marc's tender manipulations. His tongue continued its explorations, sliding up her stomach, lapping up the stream of chocolate sauce.

He started on her right breast, licking up the cream, and sucking the strawberry into his mouth before taking her nipple. Electric tingles erupted inside, zinging from her aching bud straight to her core. Marc's probing fingers found her G-Spot, and she cried out as waves of pleasure washed over her.

He moved higher up her body, pulled his fingers from her, and reached over to snatch the other strawberry from her left breast before it could slide down. His now fully erect cock prodded her core, as he placed the strawberry between her lips. He pulled himself up her torso, and his cock slid into her folds, as his lips claimed hers and the juicy fruit they held.

Vicky bit and chewed, as she tried to rid her mouth of the strawberry to fully accept his urgent kiss. His shaft rammed to the hilt inside her and sent a shock of desire coursing through her core. Sweet, chocolaty sensations filled her senses, as her channel quivered around his pulsing shaft.

The cream still on her breasts, melted in the raw heat of their passion, slicking her torso as Marc began to piston in and out of her channel and slide along her body.

Out of control, Vicky's core quaked as Marc's strokes became deeper and more urgent. An orgasmic tide rose inside, threatening to wash her over the edge. The sweet, cloying aromas were overshadowed by the sheer masculine musk that filled the air. Marc's eyes were intensely dark, his face a mask of concentration, as he drove into her again and again.

With one final thrust, he buried himself deep and emptied his essence into her. Stream after amazing stream pumped into her, filling her. She cried out as the tide took her over the edge, quivering and clutching at him. Her head spun in orgasmic ecstasy.

Marc collapsed on top of her, his comforting weight enfolding her like a warm blanket. She could feel his heart pumping strongly against her chest, and his warm breath on her neck.

"Wow," was all he was able to gasp out between deep breaths.

"Yeah," she answered.

Nothing else needed to be said.

Chapter 8

Fearful he was crushing her, Marc rallied the last of his strength to roll off Vicky. By the time he'd recovered his breath, Vicky was already sitting up. She grabbed the bottle of port wine and poured two small glasses full. She handed one to him and raised hers in a toast.

"Allez cuisine!"

It took Marc a moment to recognize the starting phrase from the popular TV show. "So, who won the Iron Chef Whipped Cream Battle?"

Vicky laughed. "I'd say we both did."

They clinked glasses and sipped down the sweet wine.

When he felt he could finally move enough to get up, Marc looked around. It hadn't been as messy as he'd thought. The sheets would still need changing and the food needed to be cleaned up, but first things first.

"I need a shower. Care to join me again?"

Vicky nodded and he offered her his hand to help her out of the bed. Errant drips of cream trickled from her breasts, and her hair was a damp tangle. Still, she was beautiful. His cock jerked as his mind filled with thoughts of what could happen in the shower.

As they exited room five into the anti-room they were surprised by Claudia Halverson and Ryan Priestly. The two club members were sitting naked in chairs.

Nudity was not uncommon or unexpected among members, but it was surprising to find someone waiting for them.

"Look, I know this is out of the ordinary," Ryan began, "but we were hoping to catch you before you cleaned up in there."

There had been a lot of speculation among club members as to the extent of the mess that would result, but Marc had a suspicion this was more than just wanting to see for themselves.

"We thought...if the story goes well..." Claudia let the thought linger, but Ryan finished it.

"...that you might want to write a sequel?"

He held up a grocery bag. "We'll pay you three points, and do all the cleanup, if you let us use the room and whatever food you have left over."

Marc saw Vicky's eyes widen in surprise. He laughed. How could he resist the offer? "It's all yours."

"We were thinking you could title our story *Sloppy Seconds,*" Claudia added as they rushed past, into room five.

Vicky broke into raucous laughter, and Marc couldn't help but join her. He noted Claudia pulling a bag of hot dog buns, and a bottle of mustard from their bag before the door closed. Yeah, that was one story he wanted to hear, though he doubted he'd ever write it.

Chapter 9

Vicky gasped as Marc rammed his cock to the hilt into her, pinning her to the tiled wall of the shower. The water cascaded around them, as he emptied himself once again into her. One thing had led to another as they'd washed each other and played around under the jets of water. God, the man had stamina.

He kissed her hard then gently pushed him away. "We better finish showering and get dressed before Claudia and Ryan come out."

"Ouch!" Ryan's cry reverberated through the wall. Vicky had a feeling that things weren't going as well for them in there.

She toweled off and slipped back into her clothes. Marc joined her and they left the room together, heading back toward the club room.

A sea of expectant faces greeted them. In most cases talking about what happened in one of the rooms was taboo, but this time everyone knew that Marc was going to write the story anyway, so they didn't have to be shy about asking questions.

The room hushed. It was Harvey that broke the silence. "So, how was it?"

Both she and Marc answered at the same time, with the same word.

"Sweet!"

Wicked Innocence

By Marc Stevens

Chapter 1

Candace 'Candy' Kane—yes, her parents had been that cruel—had experienced just about every sexual act she could imagine. She'd tried it all and liked most of it. Men, women, threesomes, foursomes, whips & chains, blindfolds and handcuffs, new sexual experiences drew her like a moth to a flame. But this was one thing she'd never had, and she'd be damned if she'd let an opportunity like this slip through her fingertips. She got wet just thinking about it.

Candy touched the icon on her smartphone to open the Point's club app. It was only the fourth time in the last hour she'd done so, but the clock was ticking down and this time she planned to leave the application open until the auction closed. She wouldn't get anything else done anyway, and she had a feeling there'd be a flurry of last-minute bids.

She had thirty-two points available. She couldn't imagine the bidding going over that, though the bid stood at fifteen points already, and that was just the women who didn't care if they won or not. Candy would wait until just before the last second to cast her bid. As the minutes clicked by the number stood at fifteen, then suddenly it started to jump up. Sixteen…eighteen…nineteen. With under a minute left Candy keyed in twenty-two points and crossed her fingers.

When the texts started to pile up in her inbox, she knew she'd won.

Well played – Tina

Damn you, Candy – Audrey

Be gentle – Bill W.

Tina chuckled at the antics of her friends in the club, but her core clenched at the thought of what she'd just won.

A virgin. A twenty-two-year-old male virgin. Probably the rarest person on the planet. God, she couldn't wait to get her hands on him.

Her phone rang, identifying the caller as Dr. Paul Fredericks.

"Hi Doc." Paul was the Points Club psychologist. He made sure people were mentally ready to handle what the club offered, without any hang-ups or entanglements.

"Congratulations Candy." Paul's deep voice reminded her of his sexy smile and good nature. "I'm just calling to remind you to go gentle on him tonight. You, of all people, know where he's coming from."

That she did. Candy had spent a few sessions with Dr. Fredericks prior to joining Points Club, to get her head on straight from a troubling childhood. She'd had her virginity ripped away from her before she was ready. She wasn't about to do that to someone else.

"You afraid I'm going to undo two years of therapy in one night?" She chuckled, but then got serious. "You know me better than that, Paul. I'll be just what he needs, and still get my points worth."

She could almost feel Paul smiling on the other end of the connection. "I knew I could count on you. Have fun."

Candy chuckled. "Oh, I plan to."

Chapter 2

Trevor paced and wiped his sweaty palms on his jeans. Tonight was the night. He wanted it so bad. He checked his phone, touching the app icon. His gut tightened and chills ran through his body. Twenty-two points? Was his virginity really worth that much?

Then he saw the winner's name: Candy Kane. Shit, the gorgeous blonde was incredible. Just picturing her long curls, sparkling blue eyes and full red lips, made his cock harden. He'd only met her once, when he was introduced to the club, but Candy stood out in that crowd of very beautiful people as a clear knock-out. She'd worn a skimpy dress that showed her enticing cleavage and long, toned legs to a real advantage. He'd never be able to last. Just thinking about her made him want to cum.

His phone rang and he answered it. Anything for a diversion.

"Trevor?" Doc Fredericks' soothing voice helped calm and settle him.

"Hey, Paul." Trevor took a deep breath.

"You can do this." The psychologist's voice was all business, but had a friendly tone. "Candy will be good for you."

Of course Candy would be good. Candy would be great! Trevor wasn't worried about her. What if he couldn't perform? What if…?

"Yeah, I'm sure everything will be great." Could Paul hear the lie in his voice?

"Just remember the club rules. You can back out at any time, and whatever happens in that room stays there unless afterward you want to spill your story to Marc Stevens. Candy will never tell another soul, not even me, unless you both consent."

That was a relief, and the main reason Dr. Fredericks had suggested Trevor join the Points Club.

Still, his mother's voice haunted him. *If you get a girl pregnant, like your God-damned father did to me, I'll cut your pecker off...*

The woman had never loved him, never wanted him. *I'd have aborted you if they'd have let me. Now I'm stuck with you.* He'd heard that diatribe from before he knew what an abortion was. She'd always made it clear, she'd never wanted him.

He shoved his mother's words into a corner of his mind and locked them away, as Dr. Fredericks taught him. She'd dominated him for too long, made him scared to even approach a woman.

Trevor ran away from home at seventeen and had lived on the streets, barely getting by, until two years ago when a beautiful woman named Chastity found him.

"I can feel your pain," she'd said. "You don't have to hurt anymore."

She'd enticed him into a room at one of the local motels and tried to seduce him. He'd thought he'd been ready. He'd wanted it so bad. But he couldn't perform. He froze up and went limp. God that had been so embarrassing.

But she hadn't laughed or gotten mad. Instead, she'd brought him to meet Paul Fredericks.

Two years of work with Dr. Paul, then just last week the psychologist said, "I think you're ready."

He told Trevor about Points Club. How everyone was checked out, disease free, and physically fit. All the women were on birth control, so there was no way for him to impregnate them. It would be a safe environment for him to explore his sexuality. Tonight would be his first night. Tonight he would lose his virginity.

And after tonight...well, Paul had said he would be ready to fly, and he planned to.

Trevor took a deep breath as he entered the North Point Supper Club. He had a lot of catching up to do.

Chapter 3

Candy saw him enter. Trevor's deep brown eyes were down, his cheeks were blushing red. God, he looked delicious. A curly mop of ebony hair crowned his head. His tightly fitted shirt hinted at some impressive musculature, and even the baggy jeans couldn't hide his erection. She felt her channel start to slicken just thinking about him naked and in her arms. She'd have to take it slow and stem her baser instincts, but she had a feeling this was a night they would both remember for a long time.

She wore her *little black dress of death.* Under it was a surprise. She considered herself a perfect package for Trevor to unwrap. She couldn't wait to see his face when she dropped the dress.

Tina and a couple of the other club women were gathering around Trevor, welcoming him in, and letting him know that they were sorry they hadn't won the auction. Yeah, he needed to know he was wanted, desired. Dr. Paul told her enough of Trevor's story to make her skin crawl. Tonight would be all about him, and his needs.

Yes, she was paying the points, but she wouldn't have it any other way.

"Alright, ladies, back off." She burst into the crowd around Trevor, eyeing him up and down. "This one is all mine."

She grabbed Trevor's hand and pulled him toward the door to the back rooms, sliding her club access card through the slot. The door lock clicked open, and he followed her through the doorway. No one got back here unless they were in the club.

Harvey, the Points Club manager and bartender, stood behind the bar in the backroom. Behind this chamber was a collection of special rooms the Points Club members used for their sexual liaisons. Candy had reserved room 1, a simple bedroom with a double bed, for the entire evening. She'd even taken time to redecorate it for tonight's occasion.

"Welcome to Points Club, Trevor. Can I get you something to drink?" Harvey's welcome was warm and sincere, despite the fact that he wore only cowboy boots and ass-less chaps. Thankfully, for Trevor's sake, Harvey's erect cock stayed hidden behind the bar. He'd no doubt get used to it over time, but it took everyone by surprise on their first night.

"A beer, with a whiskey chaser?" Trevor's voice cracked a little.

Candy could hear his nervousness.

"Coming right up." Harvey winked at Trevor, then looked at Candy. "The usual?"

"Sure." Candy brought her hand up and rubbed Trevor's back. Tension bristled in his shoulders. Your first night at Points Club, even for someone with lots of sexual experience, could be a little disconcerting. Trevor was probably petrified. A drink would help him unwind. She'd wait a bit before taking him back to the room she'd reserved. Rushing could complicate things.

"You doing okay, Trevor?" She found a knot in his shoulder and unconsciously started to kneed it out.

"Oh, that feels so good." Trevor visibly relaxed into her massage. His groan of relief was a bit louder than he'd probably intended.

"Hey," Allan Johnson said, sidling up to them. "Save that for the back rooms."

Trevor chuckled nervously, but Candy turned toward Allan, shooting him her most devilish grin. "Come on, Alan. You know I start whenever, wherever I want, and you've benefited from that on more than one occasion."

She was bound and determined to let Trevor ease into the situation at his own pace. She had all night, and she wouldn't mind if it took that long.

Chapter 4

Trevor tried as hard as he could to keep his hands from shaking as Candy led him toward the back rooms of the North Point Supper Club. She pushed open a door and dragged him into a small room with the number 1 on the door.

"This is the anti-room," she said. "Sometimes you'll find special clothing or instructions pertaining to the fantasy you're taking part in here."

It was essentially a dressing room, with clothes hanging rod, comfortable chairs, a makeup table and mirror. There was also a bathroom, with a large, tiled shower was off to the right. A second, closed door was in the wall to the left.

Candy turned to him and ran a finger suggestively down his chest. "Nothing else needed for my fantasy tonight. Just you." She took his hand and pulled him toward the closed door.

The next room was somewhat larger. A double bed stood against one wall, dressed in a frilly, pink bedspread. Pink curtains framed a faux-window that was just a framed picture of a cloud shrouded full moon. Posters of the Back Street Boys, *NSYNC, and Boyz II Men hung on the walls. Candy must have seen the question in his eyes.

"Ignore that." She waved a hand absently at the room then, grabbing him by the collar, dragged him into her. Her lips were soft but demanding. Her tongue pried its way into his mouth to tangle with his. Soft breasts pressed against his chest and his cock went rock hard in his pants.

He refused to shy away. His fingers slid into her hair, cupping the back of her head and he returned the kiss with intensity, probing with his tongue. Yeah, he wanted this.

Candy pulled back just a bit, her lips never leaving his, as she began to unbutton his shirt. One by one they came undone, and she slid her hands inside, across his chest and down his abdominals toward the place that ached for her touch.

She gasped as her mouth released him. "God, you're ripped. You work out?"

Yanking the shirt down his arms, she tossed it to the floor then returned to run her hands over him. Trevor stood there, not knowing if he should touch her or not. She'd paid for tonight. This was her fantasy he needed to fulfill.

"Is there something I should be doing?"

Candy's hands reached lower, cupping his erection through the coarse denim of his jeans. "Oh, you're doing it."

Her voice was throaty, sexy, and her eyes flashed pure delight.

She started to trail kisses down his chest, as her fingers pulled on his belt. Sensations he'd never felt before filled him. No woman had ever gotten this close to him. She was kissing his navel as she popped the button and pulled the zipper, letting his jeans slide down his legs. His cock fought to be released from his briefs and Candy slid her hand along the shaft, massaging it through the straining material.

Trevor wasn't sure how he compared to other guys, but Candy didn't appear disappointed. Warm, slender fingers slid under the waistband and tugged, freeing his shaft with one quick movement.

"Nice." A smile lit up her face as she wrapped one hand around his cock and weighed his sac with her other. It felt so incredible, but he feared he'd shoot right there. *Think of something else...anything else.*

He was so close, so incredibly close, and they'd just started. He was determined to give Candy everything he had.

His mother's face suddenly loomed in his thoughts, pulling him back from the edge. It was a technique Dr. Fredericks had taught him. For the first time in his life, his mother's abuse was actually helpful in this instance.

Candy's warm lips wrapped around the tip of his cock, sucking gently, as she ran her hand along the length of his shaft. She gently squeezed his balls and her tongue did a loop-de-loop around the spongy head.

Got to hold back. Don't think about it. But how could he help but think about it? A beautiful woman was kneeling on the floor in front of him, sliding his cock deeper and deeper into her mouth.

"Mmmmm." Candy's hum rippled along his cock, right to his core. She started to bob on his shaft. In and out. In and out. A tidal wave lifted within him.

"No." It was too much. He couldn't hold back the tide. "I can't...I'm sorry..."

It spilled over, streaming again and again into her mouth. She held him firm, drinking it all in. Sucking gently, she pulled the last of it from him.

Embarrassment and shame washed over him, reddening his face. He turned away as she stood to face him.

He felt her finger under his chin, pulling his head back around and up to face her. Her eyes were so beautifully blue, Trevor got lost in them. She folded her arms across her ample chest and tapped her foot. "And what exactly are you sorry for?"

He closed his eyes. She had every right to be angry with him. "I couldn't last. I wanted it to be special for you. I'll give you back your points..."

Candy shook her head. "No man *lasts* with me!"

Her declaration caused his eyes to spring open again.

"Last week I brought Harvey off in under three minutes, when he was determined to last five."

Trevor pulled his briefs up over his now flaccid cock. "I wanted it to last. It felt so good. I didn't want it to end so soon."

"End?" Candy's eyes brightened and she smiled a devilish smile. "Hell, Trevor, we haven't even started yet."

His confusion must have been evident, because Candy hugged him. "Oh, Trevor. Tonight's as much about you as it is about me. I just did that so you would last...next time, when it does matter for both of us."

She backed away from him and hooked her thumbs under the shoulder straps of her dress. Pulling them to the side, she let the dress slide to the floor. Underneath was a plain white bra, and white cotton briefs. No lace, no frills. Not at all what he'd expected.

She suddenly got coy, shy. "My fantasy tonight is that we're both virgins. Treat me like neither of us has ever had sex before."

Chapter 5

Candy's stomach churned as she thought back on that night seven years before. She'd planned it all out. Tom Schultz had asked her to the school dance. He was a pretty good friend, well built, and had sexy gray eyes. He was also a virgin, just like her. She'd decided he was the one. Some of her friends had done it...told her how wonderful it was.

Her parents were gone for the weekend. She had the house to herself. She'd even managed to get some condoms, in case Tom didn't have one.

Yes, she'd planned to lose her virginity that night...just not the way it happened.

They'd snuck out of the dance early. Tom had backed her into a dark corner of the gym and kissed her crazy. He'd even tentatively fondled her breast. He was as ready as she was.

The minute she opened the front door of her house, she knew something was wrong. Loud snoring poured from the living room sofa. Uncle Dave had dropped by to crash on the couch.

Uncle Dave wasn't really her uncle. He was a friend of her father's that would drop by occasionally when he got too drunk to drive home from the tavern he frequented just a block away from Candy's home. She hated the man, and his tendency to *drop in* at the worst moments. She also hated the way he would look at her—leering and licking his lips.

Still, he appeared dead to the world, so Candy ignored him and brought Tom up to her room. They'd kissed some more, and he'd slipped his hand under her dress, cupping her core through her panties.

Candy reached into her nightstand and brought out the line of condoms. "I..."

Tom reached into his pants pocket and pulled out a condom of his own. A quirky half-smile lit his face. "Me too."

She unbuttoned his shirt and ran her hands over the tanned, smooth skin of his chest. He kicked off his shoes and dropped his pants as she slipped off her dress. They stood for a moment, just in their underwear, looking at each other. She remembered how big and hard his cock had looked straining at the thin fabric of his briefs.

"Wha...the hell?" The slurred comment came from the bedroom doorway. Uncle Dave stood watching them. He had a whiskey bottle in one hand, and he was scratching his crotch with the other.

"Get yer clothes back on, boy, and get the hell out'a here."

Tom couldn't seem to move fast enough. He'd struggled back into his jeans, then grabbed up his shirt and shoes and dashed out, leaving Candy alone...with Uncle Dave.

That same look, the one she hated so much, came back into his eyes as he took a swig of whiskey and continued to scratch his crotch. She realized she was standing there in her underwear, holding a line of condoms.

"Now, what you need, girl...is a real man..."

He advanced on her and closed her bedroom door. That night he'd torn from her what she'd planned on giving to Tom. It still hurt. The scars were still there. Dr. Paul had helped her work through it. The ways she'd used sex to cover and hide that ugly night.

She looked at Trevor, standing in his underwear, just as Tom had that fateful evening. Tonight, Candy planned to have the night she'd missed seven years ago.

She looked into his eyes, took his hand and backed toward the bed. She opened the nightstand and pulled out the line of condoms. She'd been on birth control for years, but tonight they were needed for other reasons.

"I..."

Trevor reached down and pulled a condom from his jeans pocket. "Me too."

How could he have known? But he hadn't. He needed it as much as she did. It wasn't protection from pregnancy. It was protection from their pasts.

Chapter 6

Trevor had been hesitant to pull the condom out of his pocket. He'd been assured he didn't need it...but his mother's words still haunted him. *If you get a girl pregnant, like your God damned father did to me, I'll cut your pecker off...*

When Candy pulled out the condoms his heart had warmed. There was a twinkle in her eye, as if she'd known. Maybe she had. Dr. Paul had been working behind the scenes of this night for a long time.

Candy brought her lips to his ear, kissing it gently then nibbling the lobe. "I've heard, if you use two...they're even more effective." Her whispered breath was hot on his neck.

A fresh, pure scent filled his senses as she leaned into him. It was lightly floral yet reeked of innocence. He ran his hands along the velvety smooth skin of her arms. The rush was so erotic.

Pulling her into him, he kissed her...hard. Warm, wet, and enticing, his tongue tangled with hers as they tumbled back onto the bed.

They rolled toward the center, welcoming the warmth of her embrace sending his senses reeling. They ended up with the softness of her curves beneath him. As he broke the kiss, she gasped. Doubt and innocence flooded her eyes. She was playing her part well. He needed to do his part, but this was role he was born to play.

"I won't hurt you," he rasped. "I would never hurt you. If you tell me to stop right now...I'll stop."

"No," she swallowed. "Don't stop. I want this...more than anything."

He kissed her cheek then run his hungry lips to her ear, to nibble the lobe. "So do I," he whispered.

His cock had grown hard again, and pulsed in his briefs, begging to be freed, but this time he knew he could hold out longer...give Candy everything she wanted from tonight.

Awkwardly he brought his hand up to cup her breast. It felt wonderful, buoyant yet firm. He skidded his finger along the top of the bra's cup, then pulled it down to expose one ripe, puckered nipple.

"So beautiful." He brought his finger over the peak, teasing the tight bud. She arched her back and groaned. His hand moved behind her back as she arched, working toward the bra clasp. His fingers fumbled as he realized he didn't know how to open the garment.

God, what an idiot. He should have researched it on the internet. He tugged a little, but nothing happened. He sighed and rolled over, pulling her on top of him, then admitted defeat.

"I have no idea how to get this thing off."

Her eyes melted, tears puddling at the edge. She slid her fingers into his hair and grabbed tight, dragging his lips up to hers. The kiss was passionate, consuming. How could that have been the right thing to say to bring on this kind of reaction.

***

God, he was so...virginal. Her core was sopping wet and pulsing. She wanted him so badly. She needed to calm herself. Locking down her passion, she found that lost young woman inside her. Shyly she pulled away.

"It's a skill you'll need to learn, believe me." She sat up and turned in his lap, sitting on the bed between his legs with her back to him. "There're little hooks and eyelets. Go ahead take a look."

He pulled himself up and ran his fingers along the back of the bra. Tenderly he slid fingers under and pulled. She felt the catch give and her breasts sprung free.

"How the hell do you put it on?" She could almost hear the gears grinding in his head.

"If you're a good boy, I'll show you when we're done." She smiled at his naivety.

She spun to face him, draping her thighs over his, and could tell from his crooked smile that all thought of bra mechanics had been banished by the sight of her breasts. "Do you like them?"

His eyes were wide and round, but to her surprise, he raised his gaze to meet hers. "They're incredible, just like the rest of you."

Candy had known a lot of men. Few had been able to take their eyes off her breasts when facing her. How did Trevor know just the right things to say and do?

***

Trevor wished he knew just the right things to say and do. It was all so new, and he was thankful that Candy was so understanding of his awkwardness.

He could have stared at her breasts forever. They were so marvelous. Would that be wrong? Yes, it would. He tore his gaze from her breasts and looked into her deep blue eyes. He'd mumbled something or other, but seconds later couldn't even recall what it was. He probably sounded like a babbling idiot.

"Do you want to touch my breasts?" Was that a trick question? Of course, he wanted to touch them...and hold them...and tweak the nipples...

She took his hands and placed them on her mounds. Oh God, it felt great.

***

Trevor's hands gently squeezed Candy's breasts, then rolled the nipples between his thumbs and forefingers. Lightning shot through her core with each caress. When he lowered his mouth to take one in, she felt his hot breath waft across the peak, igniting a fire in her womb. Something moved deep in her core, molten, like a flow of lava, and Candy shook in his embrace.

"God, Trevor...Oh God!"

He eased her back down to the bed, his lips never leaving her breast. His tongue dragged erotically over and around the nipple, his teeth teased and nipped.

Trevor's hand stroked the side of her breast, then continued down and across her stomach, gliding along the waistband of Candy's panties. Hesitantly he flattened his palm and slid his fingers underneath.

"Yes," she encouraged him. "Touch me. Touch me there."

Fingers slid over her mons and down along her folds.

His eyes sparkled. "You're so warm...so wet."

She was. Trevor had her panting as his fingers manipulated her, sliding inside and along her folds, nudging the tender nub of her clit.

He pulled his fingers out and moved down to hook the waistband with both hands. The loss of his touch left her wanting more. She lifted her butt as he slid the soaked panties off her legs.

Candy sighed as his touch returned. Questing fingers slid into her channel. His eyes were mere inches from her womanhood, taking it all in. Would he?

Suddenly his mouth descended, his tongue licking up her entrance and across her clit. "You taste amazing."

For a novice, he sure seemed to know what he was doing down there. "Are you sure you're a virgin?" she managed to get out between pants. God, he was driving her crazy.

"I researched a lot on the internet." He plunged two fingers into her, twisting up and under, finding that incredible spot most men never discover. "I just couldn't believe it could be this cool."

"Oh, oh, oh!" A wave a passion swept over Candy and she writhed under his manipulations. His lips returned to her clit, sucking the bead into his mouth and running his tongue over and around it. Quivering in the clutch of an erotic high, Candy let lose a screech.

Trevor pulled back. "Was that good or bad?"

Candy was panting so hard she could hardly talk. "Good...very good...don't stop!"

Trevor dove back in. Two fingers pumped in and out of her channel as his tongue danced on her clit. Erotic waves rolled through her, as passions rose to new heights. Just when Candy thought she couldn't get any higher, Trevor reached up with his free hand and ran a finger across the nipple of her breast, then lightly pinched.

The dam burst. Candy was lost and the world spun around her. Like a volcanic eruption, her orgasm rolled, rocking her to her core. She lost all control of her muscles. She shook and jerked with every touch of Trevor's fingers, every caress of his tongue, until finally she collapsed back on the bed exhausted.

"Wow," Candy gasped. "I want the URL of every one of those web sites you used for research."

Trevor smiled at her, still kneeling between her legs. "All that and we're still virgins."

He was still playing along, and she loved it. She also noted the bulge in his briefs.

She sat up and hooked her fingers over the waistband of his shorts. "Well, it's definitely time we changed that."

His cock sprang out strong as she yanked down his briefs. Long, thick and dripping with passion. "Yeah, I think you're ready."

Chapter 7

Yes, he was ready—ready to leave all the baggage behind. This wonderful woman had broken the spell of the wicked witch that was his mother. No longer would he see his mother's face, hear her hurtful words. When he thought of sex, this is what he would think of. Pure, erotic, incredible.

Candy held up a condom, her eyes asked the question. "Do you know how to use one of these?"

He gulped. "I think so. And I want to protect you."

Her heart fisted in her chest.

He took the packet from her and tore it open, then unrolled the latex sheath over his erection.

His cock pulsed proudly, now sheathed in blue, as he prepared to enter her channel and break the last remaining bonds of his old life.

"Fuck me, Trevor. Fuck me like a whore," she said.

Trevor shook his head. "No, Candy. Not like a whore. Like a virgin."

He wasn't sure where the fantasy had come from, but he could feel deep down, Candy had some issues of her own to work out.

He positioned his cock at the entrance of her channel, sliding it along the wet lips, before slipping just the head into her. "Now, you tell me if it hurts, and I'll stop. I promise."

Slowly he eased into her, the feeling incredible. Every nerve along his shaft was quivering in response.

"You could never hurt me, Trevor." Her eyes glistened, rimmed with tears.

***

Trevor was giving her everything. The whole experience. She couldn't thank him enough. It was

75

worth ten times the points she'd paid. His cock pulsed strongly, and she clenched around it as it slid slowly into her.

"Yes, Trevor, yes. It doesn't hurt at all. It feels so good. Please...harder."

He pulled back, almost all the way out, then pushed in again, this time with force.

"Oh! Yessss!"

A tide of passion started to rise within her. Once again, she was that young girl in her room, experiencing love for the first time with someone who really cared for her. Carefully but insistently, Trevor built the tempo gliding in and out of her, as the fires ignited within.

It had never felt like this. She'd long ago closed her mind to passion, her body to feeling. She'd done things— extreme things—just to feel something...anything. As the tempo built, her body clenched, and like a phoenix reborn in fire, passion erupted throughout her core.

"Oh God!" she screamed. "Oh God!"

Trevor paused, confused by her outpouring.

"No, don't stop. Don't you dare stop."

The heat was back in his eyes. He pulled out and slammed into her, causing lightning to rattle her core. Thunder rumbled in her ears and waves crashed upon the shores of her soul.

Released. She cast off the chains that had bound her and became once again a sexual being. It wouldn't last. It couldn't, but Trevor was giving it his all, holding back his own flood to give her everything he had.

"I can't..." he cried. She felt him grow within her as he plunged deep one last time and ejaculated his seed. Gush after gush matched the wave upon wave that flowed over her, drowning her in passion. Her body quaked, erupting in an orgasm that left her weak and drained.

Sweat drenched, Trevor collapsed on her. His comfortable warmth and weight, like a blanket of protection that brought healing to her shattered soul.

***

Trevor rolled, using the last of his strength move his mass off Candy. He didn't want to crush her. The bedding was a mess, but he managed to throw a cover over them as Candy snuggled into his chest.

He'd done it. Put his childhood, and all its madness behind him. A new sexual lifetime stretched before him to the horizon.

They started to talk, comparing the horrors of their childhoods, and taking comfort in the warm, friendly, and accepting arms of each other. Playfully they touched and caressed each other as they talked into the evening.

"This was nice," he said with a sigh after a long silence. It seemed they had talked each other out but seemed loath to leave the warmth of the bed.

Candy wiggled in his arms and playfully licked his nipple. "I'd like to do that again sometime."

Trevor felt his cock jerk at the suggestion. "How about right now?" he asked, then raised her chin and captured her lips.

He had a lot of catching up to do.

Poolside Tryst

By Marc Stevens

Chapter 1

Tina Atkins looked at the clock on the wall of her work cubical as her hand inched under the hem of her skirt. God, would this day never end? Slipping her middle finger under her panties, she plunged it deep into her damp reaches while thumbing her clit. She needed release. God, she needed a man...a young man.

Oh yeah.

Sure, she was probably entering 'cougar country.' Trevor was only twenty-two years old, while Tina was a ripe, old twenty-nine, but the kid was so ripped and so right for the fantasy Tina had playing through her head.

How he'd remained a virgin until just a few weeks ago was a mystery. Girls should have been falling all over him. In any case, that phase of his life was over. He'd been working his way through the Points Club women at a pace that told everyone he was making up for lost time. Well, he was all Tina's tonight and she considered eight points a bargain for what she had in mind.

Mr. Thompson, her boss, dropped another pile of files on her desk, while trying to hold in his beer gut. Frank Thompson was the most junior executive at Waverly and Lowe, the advertising agency that employed Tina. She was doubtful he'd ever make it further up the ladder at the company. He just fumbled too many clients.

And as his secretary, it had made Tina lok bad as well. She'd done her best to save his ass on numerous occasions, but the man was his own worst enemy and seemed destined to fail. It wasn't that he didn't work hard; he just didn't seem to have what it took to make it in advertising.

Tina, on the other hand, knew she was more than qualified to move up. She'd talked to Mr. Waverly just that morning.

"Find a client, bring me a campaign, and then we'll talk. But for God's sake, don't let Frank Thompson know you're looking to scavenge clients." It was as close to an opportunity as she would get around here. Now she just had to find someone with a product to promote…someone off Frank's radar.

"See if you can get these done before you leave." Frank said, tapping the pile of files.

She sighed. Well, at least she'd know what clients she couldn't approach.

Frank must have been planning on working late tonight. He always tried to get her to stay a little later, on the nights he worked late.

But tonight, nothing was keeping her at the office past quitting time. She had a date with a stud that she planned to keep.

Luckily, Tina had suspected this might happen and she had a strategy in place. She reached into her desk drawer for the Overtime. Form, then patted the pile of files. "This is not going to happen without some hefty overtime."

Tina knew there was nothing in those files that needed immediate attention. He just wanted her to stay and work late so he could flirt with her after hours. He'd never be able to have the overtime authorized because he'd have to justify it to his bosses.

He'd been taking advantage of her good nature long enough. Of course, he would offer to buy her dinner after, as *compensation* for her hard work and dedication. *Yeah, right.* He just wanted to get into her pants.

While she had been flattered by his attention at first, it was getting a little out of hand. And why would she spend her night with an out-of-shape, middle-aged man when she had a hot, young stud waiting for her.

Frank harrumphed, then handed back the form. "I guess these can wait until tomorrow."

Bingo! And now, hopefully, this ugly little phase of her life was over.

She checked the time again. Just one hour to go. Her eyes drifted to the shopping bag on the edge of her desk, and the things she'd picked up over her lunch hour for tonight. Her thighs clenched. Fuck advertising, tonight was going to be about awesome sex with a hot, young stud.

Chapter 2

Trevor arrived at Dr. Paul Fredericks' house a little before 6:00 pm. He'd been here numerous times for his sessions over the past two years, but tonight was all about fun. All about sex.

Tina was a crazy beautiful woman and Trevor's cock hardened just thinking about her. An athletic build with some soft, sexy curves. Nice high breasts that drew his eye constantly. He hadn't seen her naked yet, but he was looking forward to that.

Still, he had a role to play tonight. This was her fantasy, and she was paying the points. Maybe her fantasy didn't have her undressing for him.

No matter. This was Points Club. Sooner or later, he'd probably get to see everyone naked.

He sighed. How had he lucked into such a great situation?

The house was large, but not ostentatious. Dr. Paul lived here and had his office here as well. For two years, Trever had come here for therapy to deal with some personal issues that had kept him celibate his entire life up to that time.

Thankfully, that phase of his life came to an end a few weeks ago thanks to the luscious Candy Kane.

Trevor sighed. Yeah, Candy and the Points Club had revealed a whole new world for Trevor.

He'd spent a few more nights with Candy, paying back most of the points she'd paid him for his virginity. Then she'd encouraged him to open up to the other women of the club.

He had, and with some incredible results.

Tonight, Trevor would focus his full attention on Tina Atkins and earn some points in the process. Points he could use to start living his own sexual fantasies. He had more than a few built up over the years.

Dr. Paul often let Points Club members use his home, especially the swimming pool area and guest room, for their sexual fantasies. In his therapy sessions, Trevor had often heard him say, "Sex is good for you...and lots of sex is better."

After the last two weeks, Trevor couldn't agree more.

The instruction sheet lay on the dresser of the guest bedroom. This fantasy would require some acting, but the instructions were simple: *Naked, in the pool.*

Trevor slipped out of his clothing and made his way to the swimming pool. A high security fence kept the area private, which was good. He was no exhibitionist and having sex outdoors was going to be a new experience for him. Hopefully his old phobias wouldn't inhibit him.

Thank God, Points Club was a safe environment. If he couldn't perform for any reason, he could back out at any time. No harm-no foul.

Still, today he wanted to hit a home run.

White fluffy clouds drifted across the azure sky, and the bright sun had the flooring hot as he padded barefoot across the tiles.

It wasn't so hot he had to run, and he knew the water in the pool would be cool. Looking down at his erect cock, Trevor thought that cold water would probably be a good thing. If just thoughts of Tina were making him this hard, the real thing, soft and warm in his hands, would probably bring him off far too early.

He moved to the diving board and executed an acceptable dive into the cool waters. The shock had its desired effect and he broke the surface, taking a few laps to keep his mind off sex. Not an easy task. Tina would be arriving any minute.

Just think about swimming, damn it!

Chapter 3

Tina pulled into Dr. Paul's driveway and parked her Chevy Malibu next to Trevor's rusting F-100 pickup. She noted the pizza delivery sign on the hood. Yeah, the kid didn't have a lot of money, but with his good looks and new confidence, Tina had a feeling he'd already bottomed out and was making his way back in the world.

It made her think about her own career choices. She'd been stuck in her dead-end job for far too long. She'd developed skills over the past few years that could put her ahead and into a job that would be fun and challenging. Sure, she lived comfortably and had a little money in the bank, but she certainly didn't look forward to going to work each day. It was time to think about getting out of her rut. She needed to find that client who would take her from lowly secretary to account executive at the firm.

Well, she'd worry about that after she'd finished with Trevor. God, she was so wet just thinking about him. She placed the shopping bag on the dresser and spotted Trevor's clothes piled on a chair. On top of the worn jeans and T-shirt was a green pair of boxer briefs.

Well, that answers one question.

Tina chuckled as she stripped and put on her special purchase, a sexy black string bikini. It was time to get into character. Tonight, she was rich...entitled. And Trevor was only a servant, a pool boy. A very naughty pool boy who she was about to catch swimming naked in her pool.

She exited the door to the deck and caught a glimpse of Trevor's awesome backside as he glided away from her, across the water. Lean, athletic...built for sex. She couldn't keep her eyes off his ass. She had a thing for guys with ass cheek dimples, and Trevor's were quite pronounced.

Powerful muscles propelled him through the water, flexing and bulging in all the right places. God, this was already worth the eight points. She could watch that marvelous backside for hours and never tire of it, but she was more than ready to move things along.

"Trevor!" She tried to put a bite in her tone. "What are you doing?"

His head popped up out of the water, and Tina had to bite her lip to keep from laughing at his expression.

"Ms. Atkins!" His look showed authentic surprise and horror. The young man was a consummate actor. Tina threw herself into her role. It was, after all, her fantasy.

"You're supposed to be cleaning the pool, not frolicking in it." She managed to keep from smiling. She was rich, entitled, and a servant...a *servant*...dared to swim in her pool! It was completely out of character for her. Yet, deep down, it felt good to be in charge. To be the boss. "Get up here, young man, right now!"

Trevor climbed out of the pool, his head down in shame, his cock erect and rigidly pointing at her.

"And naked. The very nerve. I should have you dismissed immediately."

He stuttered and stammered, playing his part so well. "Please, Ms. Atkins. I need this job...don't fire me...I'll do anything..."

A feeling of power washed over Tina. Was this how Frank Thompson felt, bossing her around? She'd never been in charge of anyone before.

She put her hand under Trevor's chin and raised his head so she could look him in the eye. Raising one eyebrow she cocked an evil smile.

"Anything?"

Chapter 4

It was a part Trevor could identify with. If Mrs. Wilson at Mama's Pizza House threatened to fire him, he'd have to grovel and beg. He needed that job...for now.

But not for much longer. Trevor had plans.

It was a surprising bonus he'd gotten from the members of Points Club. *Confidence.*

Confidence in himself and the project he'd been playing around with for almost a year. Without his new friends, Trevor knew he never would have moved forward. Now somehow, he felt he could accomplish anything he set his mind to.

That included pleasing Tina Atkins and taking part in her fantasy.

"Yes, Ms. Atkins, anything," he said, looking her straight in the eye. She had these amazing green eyes that could capture a man's gaze and lock him in, though with the sexy black bikini she was wearing, Trevor found his eyes drawn to other parts of her body as well.

The swell of her breasts in the barely-there top, and the erect nipples pressing against the thin material, were enough to drive any sane man crazy. Trevor had to fight the urge to reach up and palm the perfect sized mounds.

She turned, taking the temptation from him, only to present her tempting ass, minimally covered by the small triangle of fabric. The bikini was temptingly sexy, and left little to the imagination, yet Trevor longed to see this woman in all her naked glory.

Then she offered him just that.

"Take off my suit."

Her tone was perfectly imperious and commanding.

"Ms. Atkins?" He kept his voice meek.

"You heard me. Take off my suit. Start with the top. Just pull that tie in back."

He reached up for the tie, then stopped.

"Ms. Atkins, I don't know if this is proper. Your husband…"

Tina Atkins was not married, yet the instructions had stated tonight she was the entitled, trophy wife of a powerful millionaire. Trevor's role was that of a poor pool boy, trapped by a powerful woman. He found himself looking forward to the role.

"My husband is not here. You are. Do it!"

She accentuated the last two words and Trevor pulled the tie releasing the bikini top. As it fluttered to the ground, Tina crossed her arms. "Now the bottoms."

Two ties, one at each hip, beckoned him. A pull on each, had the scrap of fabric coming loose in his hands. Gloriously naked, Tina didn't even look back at him as he gawked at her incredible ass. She simply took two steps forward and grabbed a bottle of suntan lotion off one of the poolside tables.

"I do so hate tan lines. Oil me."

She handed him the bottle and settled herself face down on a padded chaise lounge.

Trevor knew he was in trouble. Pre-cum seeped from his throbbing cock already, and she was asking him to run his hands all over her tempting body. He'd never be able to hold it.

***

Tina knew she was testing Trevor's limits. A young man so new to the sexual experience would have very little staying power. She'd talked with some of the other women he'd been with in the club.

"Get him off early, and he'll come back fast and strong," Candy told her. "But make sure you let him know it's okay."

The woman's protective stance had surprised Tina. She'd never thought of Candy as particularly maternal, yet she'd practically adopted Trevor after their first encounter. Something special must have happened between them that night she'd taken Trevor's virginity.

She knew Marc Stevens had written about that night. She would definitely have to pick up that book.

Trevor was an incredible young man, and he was certainly easy to like.

His hands glided over her body, starting on her back, spreading the lotion. Occasionally his erection would nudge her as he worked the opposite side of her body. Long, thick and rock hard, Tina looked forward to having him inside her, and she wanted it to last. So, she planned to do what was needed.

His hands moved across her butt and down her legs, massaging in the sun-warmed lotion. Oh yeah, she needed more fantasies like this. A naked massage in the open sun. It felt decadent and luxurious.

When he finished with her feet she flipped. His cock was pulsing and pre-cum glistened on the tip. Trevor's unfocused look told her of his intense concentration.

"Oh!" she said. "Well, we simply must do something about this."

Reaching up she grasped his cock. Trevor's eyes went wide.

"Come for me, Trevor." She gave his shaft a jerk. "I want you to come all over my stomach and breasts."

Trevor groaned and shot hot streams of his seed across her torso. Jet after steamy jet, he emptied himself on her. The look of worry that crossed his eyes was genuine. "Tina...I..."

"Shh," she said and shot him what she hoped was a reassuring wink. "It was just what I wanted."

Tina ran a finger across her stomach through the wetness and brought it to her lips. She'd tasted lots of guys, all of them different. This one tasted of salt...and innocence.

She rose from the chaise and took his hand. "Swim with me."

She led him to the pool and dove in. The cool waters surrounded her, waking her body from the drowse she'd fallen into under the warm sun and Trevor's hands. Invigorated and refreshed she surfaced to find Trevor right beside her.

"What now, Ms. Atkins?" He was attempting to get back into character. Tina laughed and lunged into his arms, kissing him and dragging him under water. His lips never left hers as they dropped toward the bottom of the pool. Wrapping his strong arms around her, he kicked off the bottom, sending them toward the shallow end of the pool where they could stand.

As they broke the surface again, Tina broke off the kiss and laughed. "You gave me just the fantasy I wanted. To hell with pretending I'm rich, let's have some fun."

It was her fantasy, and her prerogative. She swam over to the edge of the pool and turned to face him. "Have you ever gone down on a woman?"

He nodded. "I did some with Candy, but I think I have a way to go before I'm any good. Doing it was way different than watching it on the internet."

"Well, let's give it another try." Bracing herself on the wall of the pool, Tina kicked one leg up and draped it over Trevor's shoulder, then brought the other leg up and over as well. "Look at it...take your time."

A crazy smile filled his face as he ran a finger down her opening.

"Okay, now take your tongue and retrace that path back up."

Without hesitation, Trevor dove in, licking a trail up her folds. Tina felt her clitoris expanding in anticipation, and when his tongue hit it, a bolt of pleasure shot straight to her core.

"Oh yeah," she moaned.

He then ran his tongue explanatorily around her nub, causing more sparks to fly and eliciting another moan from her. The juncture of her legs was suddenly alive with sensation as he moved down to drag his tongue up her folds once again, this time, probing deeper. The slight stubble of his five o'clock shadow rasped across her quivering thighs and as he reached the top once again, he sucked her swollen clit into his mouth, flicking his tongue across the tip. At the same time, he shot two fingers deep into her channel.

The pleasure was close to unbearable. "Oh God, Trevor, that's good. I don't think there's anyone on the internet better than you."

"Mmm, mmmm." His responsive tone was in the negative, but the vibration on her clitoris was definitely positive, causing a new wave of passionate sparks to fly through her. As she writhed in pleasure, she lost her balance and her legs slipped from his shoulders. She tumbled into the water with a splash.

Trevor tried to catch her and ended up with a face full of water.

"Sorry," Tina gasped, still in the throes of orgasm. "Maybe this wasn't the smartest place to teach you cunnilingus."

He came up sputtering but smiling. "I liked it."

Chapter 5

God, he'd loved it. Tina tasted amazing, and the way she'd reacted...well, it certainly had made him hard again.

"Come on," she said taking his hand and pulling him toward the steps. "Let's take this to the bedroom."

They toweled off and went into the house, again to the room he'd undressed in. His clothes were still there, but now hers were as well. Tina flopped onto the bed and spread her legs. "Now, do that again. Please?"

Trevor was only too happy to *do that again.* And again and again and again! He knelt on the bed and crawled between Tina's legs. With the exception of Candy, he hadn't a chance to examine a woman's private parts this close. Tina was amazingly soft and slick as he ran his finger once again along her folds. There were differences between the two, subtle, but real. *So, all women aren't the same down here.*

It made sense. Men certainly had their differences in size and shape. Why wouldn't women?

The musky scent was enticing and sensual, drawing his cock to rigid attention. He moved in closer as she spread wider to accept his face. Trevor pushed his tongue deep, taking in the intoxicatingly sweet taste of her, savoring the flavor as he moved up toward her clitoris.

Again, different than Candy, but no less wonderful.

Her nub was erect, like an excited nipple, and his mouth treated it as one. He flicked and teased as he once again pushed two fingers into her channel.

"Oh my..." Tina's body was quivering. "Oh my!"

Candy had said he was good at this. Well, he had done an indecent amount of *research* on the internet. He really didn't know if he was all that good at it. Maybe other guys were just bad.

He dragged his fingers along the upper wall of her channel. Over the past weeks he'd learned that sometimes women had a spot...

"Ahhh!" Tina cried out. "Yes, right there!"

Remembering his poolside experience, Trevor sucked in Tina's clit and began softly humming to vibrate it.

Chapter 6

Oh my god. Oh my God. Oh. My. God!

Who was teaching whom what? This boy had just graduated with honors, Phi Beta fucking Kappa!

Tina could barely contain the waves of pleasure that careened through her core. She heard someone cry out in blissful pleasure. It was probably her.

Fuck yes, it had been her! And with good reason.

Suddenly, air became an issue. She couldn't breathe; she had no control over her body. A powerful orgasm rumbled through her, leaving her raw and wasted. She gasped for air, as Trevor pulled back.

Tina was left suddenly vacant, wanting more yet doubting she'd survive it.

"Was that okay?" Trevor asked.

"Yes," she gasped, then bit her lip and closed her eyes as another wave of pleasure washed over her. *Holy fucking cow that was good.*

When she was finally under control again, she opened her eyes and looked at him, adding, "We'll probably have to practice that a lot more, though."

Oh yeah. A lot more!

He crawled over her leg and kissed his way up her body, stopping only to ravish her breasts with his mouth and quick fingers. She felt his erection against her thigh, pulsing hard, as he continued up her neck to place one final, passionate kiss on her lips. She tasted herself on his lips and found it incredibly erotic.

The kiss was long and deep, igniting a fire in her core and fueling a wave of passion. She gasped for air when he broke it off. Those lips seemed to work magic wherever they roamed.

"Is there anything else you want me to do?" he asked innocently, his hand still palming her breast.

God yes!

She reached down and wrapped her fingers around his erection. "I want you to put this thing in me and bang me senseless."

He smiled and nibbled her earlobe then whispered, "I think I can do that."

Trevor elbowed up and rolled between Tina's legs again. She felt his cock, thick and long, probing her channel. As he pushed in, his hand fondled her breast, and his mouth descended over the swollen nipple. His tongue and teeth dragged over the sensitive bud, and bolts of pleasure shot straight through her as his slim hips slammed his cock to the hilt inside her.

Trevor withdrew, then shoved into her again, and Tina gasped at the intensity of his thrust. His mouth never left her breast, as he continued to pump in and out. Faster, harder, deeper, Tina couldn't believe his penetration...how fully he filled her.

Okay, Allen Johnson was bigger, but Trevor certainly knew what to do with what he had. And what he had was well above average. She tried to focus on clenching around his shaft, giving it an extra hug each time he drove it into her, but slowly she lost the battle as her concentration crumbled and passion overtook her.

A tide of passion rose within her, threatening to spill over. Pounding with an intensity only youth can provide, Trevor drove into her again and again. He had endurance now, using long, deep thrusts to drive her to the edge of ecstasy. As it all erupted within her, he continued to pound, outlasting her by quite a bit, before emptying his seed into her and crashing to the bed beside her.

They were both gasping for long moments before either of them could talk.

Chapter 7

"That was so worth eight points," Tina finally managed to say.

"I feel guilty accepting any points for tonight," Trevor shot back. "I had such a great time. I feel I should be giving you points."

Tina kissed his cheek. "Nonsense. This was my fantasy, my points. I imagine you've got a few fantasies of your own you'll want to save up points for."

Trevor chuckled. "Right now, my top fantasy would be doing this all over again some night. I have a feeling you'll be getting your points back very soon."

Tina reached for her phone and brought up the Points Club app, then transferred the eight points to Trevor's account. "That's the way it works lots of times in Points Club. The points just go back and forth. If you offer, I will definitely take you up on a second go-round here, but I know Doc's pool is booked pretty steady for the next few weeks."

Trevor shifted on the bed and reached for Tina's phone. "Give me that for a moment."

Thinking he was just going to put his phone number in her contacts, Tina handed over her phone. When he returned it, there was a new icon on the display. "You taught me something special tonight. I'd like to at least give you something in return for that."

She touched the icon and a game popped up on her display. "Corporate chutes and ladders?"

"It's a business simulation game," Trevor explained. "You work your way up corporate ladders or go off and start your own business."

Tina found herself engrossed in the game. It was easy enough to play, yet challenging and deep in content. She lay on Trevor's chest and worked her way through the first few levels of the game with Trevor only needing to offer tips from time to time.

"This is fun. Where did you get it?"

Trevor smiled. "I wrote it. Just released it two days ago. I've even sold a few copies."

There was something very comfortable about lying on Trevor's chest and spending idle time together in the afterglow of sex. Usually, after a Points Club encounter, it was just *get up and leave.* Maybe enjoy a drink together at the bar and talk over what they'd done, or what they'd like to do next time.

Trevor seemed completely relaxed, yet animated and engaging when he talked about his game. He held her and absently stroked her hair and skin.

"So, you're a programmer?" The game could turn into an addiction, and Tina needed to tear her attention from it, and back to Trevor.

"I'm self-taught, but it's something I've been thinking of pursuing." He twirled a finger through her hair as they lay at ease on the bed.

Tina turned to look him in the eyes. "You should. This is good stuff."

Trevor lay back and his eyes glazed over. "I just need to find an investor and someone who knows something about advertising. I'm too broke right now to promote it."

Tina's gaze was drawn back to her phone and the game. Her character needed to make an important decision. Stay in her current job or take a chance and break out on her own. The game was good, engrossing and fun. "Hell, I'd invest in this. How much do you need?"

His eyes came alert, staring dark pools into hers. "Just enough for a good publicist...but Tina, I don't want to take advantage of this." His finger moved, pointing between her and himself.

Gears were moving inside Tina's head. "Trevor, I work at an ad agency. I can handle it all for you and front you the money to pay for it. And you wouldn't be taking advantage of me. If anything, I'd be using you. I need a strong client to promote so I can move up in my company, and Corporate Chutes and Ladders is the perfect product."

"Are you serious?" Trevor seemed dumbfounded by Tina's offer, but to her, it was the answer to both their prayers.

"It would be all legit, and above board. Paperwork, signed contracts, the works." Tina's head was already spinning with ideas on how to promote the game. "If you think about it, it's really no different than what we do in the Points club. We'll be using each other to achieve both our goals.

Trevor's excitement was evident. He nodded, taking it in, and his eyes widened. He took Tina in a sudden embrace, kissing her passionately and rolling on top of her on the bed. His cock was hard, prodding her stomach.

"I think it's an amazing idea," he said, breaking the kiss. "And if you're game, I think I'd like to spend a few points and *use* you one more time."

Tina smiled up at him. "I think that would be a great way to seal our new partnership."

Chapter 8

Two weeks later, Tina sat in the board room at Waverly and Lowe next to the president of Next Step Gaming. He'd cleaned up pretty good. The charcoal grey power-suit, baby-blue dress shirt, and gold, silk tie made Trevor look professional and drop-dead sexy. Tina had noted the young women in the office casting him looks that dripped with lust during his frequent visits over the past week.

The initial launch of Corporate Chutes and Ladders had been so successful Trevor had already paid Tina back over half her investment, with a healthy chunk of interest. He was on his way, and Tina couldn't have been happier for him. Now it was time to discuss what was next for his new Next Step Gaming startup.

The ad campaign had also vaulted her into a vacated account representative position at the company, complete with a nice, private office that she planned to drag Trevor back to after the meeting. They tended to have long, exhausting meetings where the points flew back and forth with fierce determination.

She reached under the table and ran her hand over Trevor's crotch, feeling his cock harden. A consummate actor, the only reaction he had above the table was a slight widening of his already glowing smile, but in retribution he started inching his hand up her thigh, under her skirt.

Whoever said that you couldn't mix business with pleasure...was just fucking wrong.

Sex and Lasers

By Marc Stevens

Chapter 1

"I didn't realize Points Club stuff happened much outside the club."

Marc Stevens finished typing the notes into his laptop detailing Tina Atkins sexual encounter at one of the Points Club member's private swimming pool. There were so many different rooms to discover hidden in the back of the North Point Supper Club, Marc hadn't even thought of activities outside the building.

Tina laughed. The vivacious brunette's smile was contagious. "Marc, you have no idea. Once you've been here a while, you'll realize it's happening all over town, sometimes right under people's noses." She put her hand to her cheek and whispered, "I think some people want to be caught in the act."

She waved to Maya Taylor, who was tending bar that night, to get her attention. "Maya, bring over that Club Venues List."

The thing was two pages long and listed all the places outside the North Point Supper Club that could be used for Points Club activities.

One just kind of jumped off the page at Marc. "Laser tag?"

Tina's eyes lit up. "Naked laser tag. It's a blast. If you're interested, I bet I could put teams together for tonight."

Mark tried to imagine what it would be like. In the end he couldn't resist. "It sounds like it would make a great story in any case."

Pulling out her phone, Tina set up the event in the Points Club app.

Marc grabbed a slot.

There was an amused chuckle throughout the room, as word circulated among the gathered Points Club members.

"Naked laser tag? I'm so in." Ryan Priestley's shout filled the barroom.

"I'm in, if I can be on the other team," Candy Kane answered. She pointed at Ryan. "You're going down, sucka, and then I'm going down on you."

Ryan cocked his head arrogantly. "You should be so lucky."

That brought on a chorus of laughter and a few friendly side bets from the gathered members. It looked like naked laser tag was on.

Chapter 2

Tina hit the power switch inside the doorway of the massive, dark structure, and the old laser tag compound came to life. Neon glowed and lights blinked, illuminating the playing area of Nick's Laser Tag Emporium. Nick's had been the *in* place during the height of the laser tag boom, but had fallen on tough times, closing down five years ago.

Harvey, the Points Club leader and bartender, picked the place up for a song from the bank's foreclosure on the structure, and offered it to any members of the club whenever they wanted a match. Tina was one of those charged with keeping the structure maintained, so she knew everything would be in order. The outside of the building looked a bit dilapidated, giving the place an unused, derelict appearance, detouring break-ins. The inside, however, was clean, maintained and ready for some sexy fun at a moment's notice.

Candy Kane, Claudia Halverson, Ryan Priestley, Jim Burns and Marc Stevens gathered around her, as Tina went over the rules. Along with Marc, it was also Jim and Claudia's first time here.

"Everybody showers and gets naked, except for the Laser Tag harness." She held up the thin leather strap that contained two laser sensors. Harvey had spared no expense redesigning the bulky old Laser Tag Vests into something a little more comfortable and revealing. The women's harness looked like a bra-less corset, with the laser sensor centered just under their breasts. The guys got a harness that put the sensor squarely in the center of their chests.

"I'll look like He-Man," Jim joked.

Each harness also had a second sensor positioned in the small of the back.

"If you get hit, your belt will beep and vibrate, then start a two-minute timer. Immediately drop to the floor and lay still. This gives the other team an advantage while hunting down the other players.

"If you get hit, it costs you two points. If you're the shooter, you get the two points. The guns and sensors are remotely tied in with Harvey's program, so the points are awarded automatically as we play. Friendly fire still costs you, so make sure of your target before you pull the trigger. There are no *takebacks.* The points will be yours to use any way you want afterward...or even during the two minutes if you both agree."

A sly smile spread across Tina's face. "It's boys against the girls. Boys, take the far dressing room and get ready. Game starts in ten minutes."

Tina eyed Marc Stevens tight ass as he turned to follow the other men toward the far dressing room. Oh yeah, she wanted a piece of that. She'd be sure to give the erotic author something to write about if she could snag him.

[Author's note: Yeah, she told me she was really thinking that.]

Chapter 3

Ryan Priestley checked the balance on his laser gun. He couldn't wait to get Candy Kane in his sights. That sultry blonde was just begging for it, and he'd be happy to give it to her.

"The trick is to aim for their boobs, but don't get distracted by the jiggle and forget to pull the trigger." He was the only one on the guys' team with any experience. "And if either of you two noobs shoots me by mistake, there will be hell to pay."

He'd been in enough matches with new players. They tended to shoot at anything that moved. "Seriously, forget the 'whites of their eyes,' look for nipples on those beautiful breasts. Play your cards right and be careful, and you'll have one of those amazing babes paying you points to fuck them."

As the veteran, he felt it his obligation to instruct the new players, but that was the end of his pep talk. The buzzer sounded and he opened the dressing room door. "Spread out, stay in the shadows and look for your opportunity...and don't fucking shoot *me*."

The building was huge, filled with a maze of winding hallways, pillars, and bunkers, all padded with vinyl covered foam for safety and comfort. Ryan dashed toward a hallway that wound around the outside of the playing area. It would be suicide to charge directly into the middle, though he expected Marc and Jim would do just that.

"Noobs," he said under his breath, shaking his head.

He knew with a little luck, he could maneuver behind the women and take them down, using the other guys as decoys. If the noobs got shot in the process, oh well. That's the way the cookie crumbled.

Ah those ladies. One blonde, one brunette, and one redhead. Each one a beauty. Ryan would be happy banging any of them. But he was gunning for the blonde.

Candy Kane had made it clear she was going to come after him in this match. Tina and Candy had both played extensively, so the girls had a bit of an edge. Ryan was sure, though, he could even things up.

He grinned at the thought. "Heh, heh. Time to bag me some lovely ladies."

A flash of perfect ivory skin flashed across his vision. One of the girls was just ahead and to the right. Moving carefully from shadow to shadow he held his laser gun ready. A lush fall of auburn hair told him he had Claudia in his sights. His mouth watered as he eyed his target's perfect ass.

Another noob. He'd take her down first, give one of the other guys an easy win, then move on to the real challenge.

Claudia was standing straight up, her back to him. She even had a barrier to crouch behind but wasn't using it. She was the perfect target.

As he rose from his cover to sight in the sensor at the small of her back, she dropped sideways behind the barrier.

Damn.

Had she heard him behind her?

The buzzer in his sensor went off and vibrations rattled his chest. Across the room he saw Jim Burns, his laser gun extended. They'd both been shooting at Claudia, but when she dodged, Jim's shot must have struck him.

"Shit. I'm sorry," Jim called across the room as he turned to flee down a hallway. Ryan closed his eyes and shook his head as he dropped to the floor.

Two minutes out of the game. But he was down behind cover. Hopefully one of the women would still spot him. Some of the best action happened in these two-minute time-outs.

Still, Jim would have to pay him two points, so it wasn't all bad.

"Friendly fire can be a bitch." The sultry whisper came from the hallway behind him. "Then again, so can I."

Cat-like she prowled into sight, crawling on all fours toward his prone body. Her pink tongue slid out of ruby red lips. A fall of blonde hair shadowed her eyes. "May I?"

"Please do," Ryan said chuckling. How could he have gotten so lucky?

***

Claudia breathed a sigh of relief. She'd seen Jim moving in on her and dropped to the floor to avoid his shot.

"Shit. I'm sorry." What was he apologizing for? This was all part of the game, and he'd missed her anyway.

She held her laser gun close as she crawled around the padded barrier just in time to see Jim's dimpled butt cheek exiting the area through a side doorway. The scaredy-cat was on the run. She pushed to her feet to follow him.

She could only see about twenty feet down the hall, where it curved to the left. A single light bulb blinked on and off every few seconds, causing her heart to leap in her chest whenever the hallway was plunged into darkness.

She cautiously moved down the hallway, pistol ready for anything that moved. This was so intense. A thrill ran up her spine setting all her nerves on edge but also triggering her juices to flow down below. Yeah, she would definitely be doing this again...and again. The thought of catching Jim—

106

tagging him. The things she'd ask him to do. Surely, he wouldn't say no. God, she got wet just thinking about the possibilities.

The light went out again. Her heart rate quickened as she shuffled in the darkness, one hand touching the wall to feel her way, the other holding the laser gun in front of her, ready to fire. He was there, just around the corner...she could feel it.

When the light flickered back on, she saw his outline, standing at the end of the hall. She fired quickly, too quickly. It was just his shadow, he was on the other side of the hall, between the flickering light and the curving wall.

Bzzzt. Her chest sensor vibrated, indicating he'd hit her.

"Damn it!" She dropped to the floor.

"She's stunned, Bones. What should we do with her?" Jim was having a conversation with himself as he approached where Claudia lay. "Damn it, Jim, I'm a doctor not a prison guard." His voice altered as he changed characters. He was already setting the scene he wanted to play. "Then maybe you should examine her."

Jim was a huge science fiction nerd and loved to spout lines from movies and television shows. He had a lot of the voices spot on. It was easy to tell the part she'd be playing in his little fantasy.

He crouched down beside her and ran a finger along her cheek bone. "Yeah, maybe I should examine her, if she'll let me."

"God, yes!" She was ready for anything.

His finger continued down the side of her neck then trailed between her breasts, circling underneath. He cupped her right breast in the palm of his hand and ran his index finger over her puckering nipple. "She appears to have very healthy...lungs."

Claudia couldn't hold in a chuckle any longer. "You have the worst bedside manner Doctor McCoy."

Jim went down on all fours and dipped his head to suckle her left nipple. As his rough tongue slid over her tender bud, electric shocks cascaded through her core. Coming up for air he asked, "Is that any better?"

"Mmmmm. It's a good start, doctor, but I think it's making me hot."

He continued licking, crouching over her and moving down her torso, toward her navel. "I've always wanted a Claudia lollypop. So sweet."

His tongue dancing on her skin, he moved lower, lapping over her shaved mons toward her clitoris. "So very sweet."

As he moved, he swung a leg over her head, so his engorged cock swung right over her mouth.

"Oh look," she said. "I get something to lick too."

A bead of moisture leaked from the slit on the spongy head, and she raised up to run her tongue over it, tasting the salty seepage, and inhaling the musky man scent of him. She took the head into her mouth and swirled her tongue around it.

"Oh yeah, baby. Just like that."

His tongue worked lower, finding her clit and circling it. "God, you taste good."

He dove in, taking the swollen clitoris into his mouth and gently sucking.

Claudia's channel slicked with desire, as he ran questing fingers along her folds. She rose a bit to take more of his massive cock into her mouth. His sack hung almost to her nose.

Jim drove two fingers into her moist channel, and she squirmed with delight. He managed to find every erotic zone on the chart while continuing to suck and lick. Waves of unbelievable passion washed over her as he caressed and manipulated her most intimate areas.

She bobbed and sucked harder on his cock, noticing that his balls tightened around the base, as the head expand in her throat. He was getting close, but she beat him to the punch. His ministrations found just the right combination to send her over the edge. Writhing beneath him, an intense orgasm washed over her.

Jim pulled back, helping her ride the waves, slowing his caresses and pulling his cock from her mouth. She gasped for breath. "Oh my, oh my, oh my!"

Her head was spinning as she fought to control her breathing.

He crawled back around so he was kneeling beside her again. "I think she needs some mouth-to-mouth resuscitation, Captain."

His lips descended to hers, and she grabbed him around his neck, drawing him in. Warmth spread from her core to fill her completely.

As they kissed, her sensor beeped, indicating the two minutes were up and she was free to break it off to get back to the game.

Fuck that. This cost her two points, and she was going to get her money's worth.

She was right where she wanted to be. They rolled on the floor kissing, and she could feel his hard cock pulsing between them. Breaking the kiss, Claudia replied in her best Scottish accent, "You're going to have to reseat that dilithium rod, Captain. I've got to have more power!"

Jim chuckled as he rolled her onto her back, spread her legs and plunged his cock deep into her moist channel. His eyes blazed. "Warp factor six." He pulled out and plunged again.

God, the feeling of that massive cock pounding into her. She could see him straining to hold back his orgasm.

He quickened his pace, pumping into her full force. "Warp factor seven," he grunted out through clenched teeth."

With one final plunge he came, shooting strong spurts into her. Warmth and passion washed over her, as he collapsed in her arms.

"Reactor overload?" she asked.

"And then some," he answered chuckling.

Chapter 4

Marc Stevens crept through a hallway that sloped upward. He'd already heard two buzzers go off. Presumably two down, which meant four occupied. That left him and...whom?

"It's just you and me, author man." Tina's voice drifted up from somewhere below. "You got what it takes?"

Marc had played a bit of laser tag in his youth. He'd also played some paintball with his friends. But he wasn't sure any of that prepared him for this. One shot. One lucky shot was all it took. Still, did it really matter who won?

He had points to spare, and Tina would make the encounter interesting enough to write about, he was sure of that.

Still, he preferred to play to win. He knew Tina would. God, he wanted her so bad his cock twitched just thinking about her. He'd written about her sexual adventures a couple of times, heard her describe events and painted pictures in his head. He'd imagined what it would be like to fuck her many times. Now he had his chance.

"Come get some," he hollered back, then sprinted up the ramp and into the small room at the top.

There was a myriad of objects to hide behind, all padded with soft foam and covered in vinyl. There were only two hallways leading out of the room. He chose a hiding spot with a view of both. Listening hard for footsteps, he waited for Tina to appear. She was more familiar with the maze of tunnels and rooms, and probably knew exactly where he was. His only hope was to keep watching and listening. Let her come to him.

Poom. Something landed on the padded floor behind him.

Bzzzt. As Marc spun to see what it was, his sensor vibrated and Tina said, "I'm here to get some."

"How the hell . . ." But as Marc fell to the floor, he noted the circular opening in the ceiling above. An entrance to the room he'd completely missed.

"I know," Tina said. "Totally unfair. I know every inch of this maze." She crouched down beside him, her incredible breasts just inches from his mouth. "But it's your first time, so I'll be gentle."

***

Candy had Ryan just where she wanted him. The man was arrogant, overbearing, and cocky, but he had the body of a god. She had no doubt he'd plotted some dominant fantasy for whoever he'd planned to snag tonight.

Not that Candy minded a little domination. Played right, it could be incredibly erotic, and from what she'd heard, Ryan knew how to play it right.

Still, she hated to let him get the upper hand all the time, and tonight she'd been lucky to come up behind him. She'd had him in her sights and was about to fire when his sensor went off, hit by Jim's stray shot. She felt no guilt taking advantage of the situation. She'd have had him anyway.

"Poor baby. Do you want to back out on this one?" She was poised over his body and reaching toward his balls. "May I?"

"God, of course."

"I'll tell you what. I'll give you a chance. You've got a little under two minutes left to on your timer." She slid her hand up his shaft and felt it jerk in her hand. He was already close. "You hold off until your back in the game, and I'll let you shoot

112

me, point blank, and you can do whatever you want to me."

Candy trailed kisses and nips down his stomach, heading for his pulsing cock.

Ryan had a reputation as a fast trigger. She knew he didn't stand a chance.

Chapter 5

Ryan was in deep shit. Candy was legendary with her mouth and tongue. Everyone knew it. She'd blown guys in under thirty seconds. The things she could do...

But it was a challenge he couldn't turn down. "You're on."

He gritted his teeth. It was only two minutes. He was sure he could hold out.

Candy's silken lips slid down his cock, her tongue already at work on the underside of his shaft. God, it felt incredible. Her hand slid down to cup his balls and massage the base of his shaft.

Tightening her lips, she pulled back up his pole and tortured the sensitive, spongy head. The way her hand manipulated the base of his cock had him already fighting hard to hold back his orgasm.

"Oh God, Candy. Where the hell did you learn to do that?"

He needed a distraction, something to take his mind off his cock and the incredible things Candy was doing to it. Something...anything.

But nothing came to mind. His entire being was focused on his groin, and the woman just kept on it. Pleasing it. Heightening the sensitivity by the second. How was he ever going to hold on?

As her fingers stroked, her lips and tongue attacked, and Ryan felt his balls tighten. It had to be at least two minutes. Why hadn't his sensor dinged? The damned thing had to be broken.

Then Candy took his cock deep, her throat closing around the head like a vise. It was all over. There was no holding back the intense erotic pressure, and his dam burst, shooting stream after stream of cum into Candy's eager mouth.

She never lost a drop, as she sucked him dry. He was spent, gasping for air.

Hell, forget what he'd been planning for Candy. Even his fertile imagination couldn't have dreamed up anything a satisfying as what Candy had just done to him.

Still, it rankled. He was sure he'd lasted longer than two minutes.

"I think my sensor's broken," he managed to say between gasps. "I know I—"

Ding. The damn sensor chimed, denying his claim.

"I don't think so, tiger." She gave the head of his wilting cock one last kiss.

***

Candy felt oddly satisfied. She hadn't really gotten any sex, but she hadn't lost any points either. The night was a wash, sexually speaking...at least so far. Getting one up on Ryan had been a real turn on though, and the night was still young.

I think I'll head back to the club and see what's left to pick up.

There was always action to be had at the North Point Supper Club, right up to closing time. Hell, at the end of the night, Harvey was always looking for a tumble after hours, and that guy knew how to satisfy a lady.

Chapter 6

A wicked smile played over Tina's lips as she ran her hand down Marc's chest. His cock was standing up, hard and strong, and she wrapped her fingers around it. Marc groaned in ecstasy as she ran her hand up and down his shaft. "You are okay with losing to me, aren't you?"

Marc realized he still had some leverage over the situation. "You're afraid of how I'm going to write up this little altercation?"

Tina nodded.

"I'm a bigger man than that," he said. "It's going in the story exactly as it happened. You won, fair and square. I'm all yours for the next two minutes." Then he winked and added, "Maybe even longer."

Her hand continued to pump his cock. "Well, you are a very *big* man."

She bent down and kissed him, adding an additional erotic element to the mix. Marc's head spun and she intensified her kiss, pressing her breasts against him, her nipples hardening against his chest.

He wrapped his left arm around her and brought his right hand up to cup her breast, stroking the erect nipple. Tina groaned as she kissed him.

She broke off the kiss and pulled back a bit. "I wouldn't mind if you sucked on that."

"Yeah?" His mouth watered as he brought it up toward Tina's breast. "I wouldn't mind that either."

Tina's breasts weren't overly large. In Marc's estimation they were just right, and proportional to the woman, enhancing her appeal. The nipple stood up straight and hard under the assault of his tongue, and the salty silkiness of her skin felt and tasted amazing.

He glided his hand up her back and under her soft brunette tresses to pull her closer, sucking gently as she moaned in his embrace.

"Oh yeah," she gasped. "That's the stuff."

While keeping her breast accessible to Marc's mouth, Tina swung a leg over his chest, straddling him. "I need you inside me. You've got me just dripping wet."

She sat back, sliding his pulsing shaft into her slick channel. She was tight, but so wet it slid into her easily. He moved his hands to support her thighs as she began to rock and grind.

"Oh," she gasped as he felt his cock grow even larger inside her.

She pulled up, and he lost contact with her breast. Sitting up straight she began to piston, up and down on his shaft. Her breasts bounced attractively, easily capturing his attention. The sight and feel were so incredible, he felt his control about to burst.

"Don't come yet," she pleaded. "I'm not quite there."

What control did he have? The woman had him right on the edge.

Think of something else. Anything else.

Alligators, puppy dogs...Mrs. Rayburn, his 7th grade math teacher.

One squared equals one. Two squared equals four. Three squared equals nine...

Marc felt his control return as Tina pumped faster on top of him. Even as she intensified and quickened her thrusts, he pushed his orgasm away using the tediously learned square root tables from his seventh-grade math book.

Mrs. Rayburn always said he'd someday find a good use for square roots. Turned out, she was right. *I wonder if this was what she had in mind?*

Chapter 7

Candy was making her way toward the dressing room when she bumped into Claudia and Jim. "So, how was it?" she asked. Their smiles told her a lot.

"Great," Jim said. "I'll have to do this again."

"Ditto," Claudia added.

Then Jim cringed. "I hope Ryan's not too pissed that I shot him. It was really not my fault. He was standing right behind Claudia when I shot at her. I never saw him until she ducked."

Candy chuckled, remembering the incident. "He'll get over it, but I would avoid him for a few days."

"I can see I'll need a lot more practice," he said.

Claudia leaned over to nibble his ear. "I'll be glad to help you."

Yeah, it seemed that things went well for these first-timers. Candy wondered how Marc Stevens was fairing. She sure hoped he would want to write about this little adventure. Everyone in Points Club was angling to get into one of his stories.

"Oh God, Oh God!" Tina's voice reached them from somewhere above.

"Sounds like Marc and Tina ran into each other," Candy said.

Jim cocked his head to listen. "I wonder who shot whom?"

Claudia laughed. "At this point, I have a feeling it doesn't really matter."

"It rarely does," Candy added with a smile. "It rarely does."

Chapter 8

"Oh God, oh God!" Tina fought for control, but she was too far gone. Marc's large, pulsing cock filled her so completely. Her core was on fire, igniting every nerve in her body, as she continued to bounce up and down on Marc's shaft. His thick rigid member had her quivering in delight and right on the edge of orgasm. Could he hold out?

Beneath her she noted Marc's face was drawn tight in concentration. God the man had control. What was he thinking?

***

Seven squared equals...Fuck! What did seven squared equal? Marc's cock begged for release. His balls were pulled tight to the base of his shaft. *Seven...fucking...squared.*

Tina's body rippled as she rode him. She rose up until only the thick head of his shaft was still inside her, then came crashing down one last time, her body quaking in orgasm. It was too much. Even Mrs. Rayburn's square roots couldn't keep back the tide that washed over him.

"Arrrg!" The cry that originated deep in his throat was more animal like than human. Losing all control he released hard, emptying himself into her, pumping again and again. His mind was a whirl of stars and color, his body completely sated.

Tina collapsed on top of him, her soft breasts pillowing on his chest. Sweat drenched both bodies. Her chestnut hair fell around his face. Velvety soft and smelling of flowers, Mark ran his fingers through the strands. Then he rolled, his cock still in her, to put her underneath him.

"That...was amazing." His lips crushed hers, in thanks for an experience he'd long remember.

Sweet and tender, she returned the kiss, nipping at his lips as he pulled back.

"Yeah," she said, still breathing hard. "We'll have to do this again sometime. Maybe a private session? Just the two of us?"

Marc raised an eyebrow. "Is that a challenge?"

Her eyes gleamed with mischief. "Mm Hmm."

Chuckling, he gave her a hug. "Oh, you are so on."

Of course, he'd have to talk someone else into helping him practice. Someone not quite as good a player as Tina Atkins.

Chapter 9

They'd carpooled together in Tina's SUV, so on the drive back to the North Point Supper Club, Marc took copious notes for the story he planned to write. Everyone shared their experiences, though Ryan was a little less than eager to give up his part of the story.

"Watch your back, Candy Kane," he said waggling his finger at her. "I will get my revenge."

"I'm looking forward to it," Candy replied, running her tongue across her ruby lips. Marc could tell it was a playful, friendly rivalry, and had a feeling that would be another story worth writing.

"Who won?" Allan Johnson shouted over the noise of the barroom as the six laser tag players entered to cheers.

"We all did, of course," Tina responded and caused amused laughter to ripple throughout the room.

As the others filtered into the crowd, Marc sought the solitude of a corner booth. He needed to digest everything that had happened. Maya brought him over a glass of his favorite wine, and his mind started to clear.

Forty-nine! The square root of seven is forty-nine.

Opening his laptop, he began to write. He had a hell of a tale to tell.

Raider of the Lost Blonde

By Marc Stevens

Chapter 1

Candy Kane sat curled on her couch, her mind ablaze with sexy, heroic images as the actor on the television screen wheeled the large wooden box through a warehouse piled high with crates. The *Raiders March* played while the credits rolled at the end of the movie.

She reached into the greasy bowl and grabbed the last few kernels of popcorn. Sliding them into her mouth and licking the butter from her fingers.

The DVD cycled to the menu screen, and she stared into the eyes of her fantasy. Indiana Jones...leather jacket, whip, fedora and all. "God, that man was sexy."

Even at his current advanced age, Harrison Ford still did it for her, though she'd be afraid of killing the old man in bed if she ever got him there.

She realized she didn't really want popcorn. What she hungered for was a handsome stud in a leather jacket and fedora, with a whip and gun at his side—toned abs peeking through his open khaki shirt.

She plunged her hand between her legs, fingering her clit and damp folds as she imagined him confronting her in a ruined jungle pyramid.

"Oh Indy!"

Candy closed her eyes and lay back, spreading her legs wider, continuing to manipulate her clit and delve deeply into her core. In her mind she saw him drop his gun belt as she ripped open his shirt to run her fingers over the tightly knotted muscle.

But the fantasy wasn't enough. She needed something real. She needed a man, and she knew just the right man for the job. Why fantasize when you can manipulate reality to suite your needs?

Thank goodness for Points Club.

She pushed Alan Johnson's number on her phone, hoping he'd answer...hoping he'd be available.

"Hey beautiful. I sure hope this is a booty call." Alan's deep sexy voice always got her juices flowing.

"You know it, love. I need a hero tonight. You available?"

"For you, kid, any time." Yeah, he was a smooth talker, but tonight that was just what she needed. That and someone who could shoot from the hip...literally.

He cleared his throat, then got all serious. "What do you have in mind?"

Candy couldn't help but smile. "Are you up for a little adventure?"

Chapter 2

The package arrived by express delivery, only a few hours after he hung up with Candy. Khakis, a worn leather jacket, high boots, and a battered fedora. It wasn't a costume. They were the real fuckin' thing—every piece. Alan just stood and stared at himself in the mirror. Yeah, he could pull this off.

It didn't surprise Alan that Candy knew people who could make things like this happen fast. The woman was amazing. But a complete, authentic Indiana Jones outfit in mere hours...and everything in his size? Alan wondered if some kind of magic wasn't involved.

"Either that or she's been planning this for a long time."

At the bottom of the box was a gun holster, but no gun. Not surprising, as they had a few fake guns in the Points Club prop room. As for Indy's signature bullwhip, well there were plenty of those in room 7.

Alan smiled, thinking about how he'd conned Tina into going in there. So many people in Points Club avoided room 7 like the plague.

He adjusted the fedora on his head and checked his reflection in the mirror. The old grandfather clock in his den chimed 7:00PM. It was time to meet Candy at the North Point Supper Club.

"Yeah, this should be fun."

Chapter 3

One last piece needed to fall into place to make Candy's evening perfect. It could have been any of a dozen men, but one, in particular, had her hoping...praying...he would be at the club that night.

Marc Stevens tended to turn his phone off when he was writing and could be a hard man to contact.

[Authors Note: Guilty.]

When Candy saw the author sitting in one of the booths, she got a warm feeling in her stomach. Still, she wasn't sure he'd agree to play a part in her scenario, especially the part she wanted him to play. She'd need to intrigue him—let him know there was a story here for him to write.

Candy ducked into the Points Club prop closet and retrieved one of the realistic looking paintball guns, filling it with a couple of red paintballs. As she exited the closet, she saw Alan Jackson just entering the club room. God, he looked breathtaking in the Indiana Jones gear.

She'd imagined it countless times. She'd gone over all the male Points Club members to find her perfect match then, settling on Alan Johnson. She'd even ordered the gear in his size. Yes, this was no spur of the moment decision. She'd been planning this fantasy for months. This morning's re-watch of the classic movie trilogy (the 4th movie didn't count, and never would in her mind) only primed the pump for this evening's activities.

Alan strode up to her, putting a bit of extra swagger in his gate. He eyed the gun and asked, "So, who do I get to shoot?"

Candy looked over at Marc. "Hopefully him."

Alan smiled. "Perfect. You think he'll write it up as one of his stories?"

"Come help me convince him. You wouldn't mind being in another one of his stories, would you?" All parties needed to agree to waive the *Do not tell* policy of Points Club and allow Marc Stevens to write about their sexual encounters.

"Oh, I'm totally good with that." Alan's hand came down to pat her on the behind, cupping her butt and lingering erotically longer than necessary before pushing her forward. The man was incorrigible. Candy liked that about him.

She noted when she'd caught Marc's attention. His eyes drifted to her breasts. Candy knew her assets, and just how to use them. Especially on men. She did have to give Marc credit, though. He managed to pull his eyes up to meet hers...eventually.

She stopped in front of the table, and felt Alan behind her, ready to back her up. That felt oddly good—Alan ready to back her up. Still, Candy was a woman who prided herself on being able to stand up for herself.

"Hey, Marc, would you mind being shot."

Marc's eyes showed his shock and surprise when he noted the gun she was holding. He raised his hands. "What did I do? What did I do?"

She had to laugh, looking down at the pistol then back to Marc. Did he actually believe the gun was real?

She shook her head. "No, this is just one of the prop paintball guns we use in role playing. I want you to play the bad guy in a scenario, but you'd need to be shot. It's just a small part to get things going, but I'll pay you two points."

Candy could see he was hesitant. She gave him her *puppy dog* eyes, the one she'd cultivated that tended to melt just about any man. "Please?"

He caved. "Does it hurt?"

Alan leaned over Candy's shoulder and said, "It stings a little, but not bad. I've shot people and been shot myself, dozens of times. It's perfectly safe."

Marc seemed to relax then. He cocked his head in the cutest way. "Is this going to be something for me to write about?"

Candy knew she had him. "Count on it."

Alan waited behind the door in the anteroom for his cue. Candy had spent the last half hour going over everything she was looking for in her little Indiana Jones fantasy. Now he just had to wait until Marc said the line, "I've been waiting for this a long time."

He chuckled and shook his head. Candy sure had a flare for the dramatic. Still, he had to admit, this was going to be fun.

It wasn't always fun taking part in someone else's sexual fantasy. Alan had taken on a number of distasteful roles over the years and turned down countless others. He also knew some of his own fantasies bordered on the bazaar. Things he wouldn't have had the guts to ask someone else to do outside the club.

That was the reason Points Club existed. You could have your darkest, craziest sexual fantasies fulfilled, and the code kept everyone quiet about it. Only recently had they lightened up on the rules and allowed Marc Stevens to write his stories about the club.

Still, there were things done here that no one would ever talk about, and things, Alan was sure, that Marc would refuse to write about even if everyone involved agreed to talk. The dark fantasies the human mind could conceive of were limitless, especially when they centered on sex.

This, however, wouldn't be one of those. Leave it to Candy to craft a fantasy tailor made for Marc's blog and stories. She'd wiggled her way into several of Marc's stories and blog posts already, and probably had read them each a dozen times.

Alan liked Candy. The vivacious blonde was sharp, and so together—one of those people who seemed to float through the world, untouched by the darkness. She always made Alan smile. He'd bedded her dozens of times over the years and always found her passionate and responsive.

While Points Club brought them all together, it also erected barriers between the members. Sex was just sex. You checked your emotions at the door. It had worked for Alan for years. Too much heartbreak, betrayal and drama had driven him from one failed relationship to another in his youth. Points Club had offered him a respite from all that.

But lately a darkness had settled in his mind. His world, so balanced and centered on sex, seemed suddenly out of sync. Something was missing. Only that morning he'd considered leaving the club, going back out into the real world and *dating* again. Then Candy had called.

He smiled. He could never say no to her. And to spend one more night walking in her fantasy world, taking her to bed, pretending he loved her. Yeah, he could do that.

Taking a deep breath, he put his ear to the door and waited for his cue.

***

Candy was backed against the wall, the heat of Marc's toned, trim body pressed against her. His hands moved possessively over her clothed body, sending sparks dancing through her core. It wasn't at all what she'd imagined when she'd plotted the scene. He truly wanted her, she could tell, and even if it was just for the sex, being wanted was something Candy craved on a base level.

"You're mine. Do you understand? Mine!" Marc was throwing himself into the role. His eyes blazed with passion. If only someone truly wanted *her* this passionately—not just her body.

He grabbed her blouse by the collar and ripped it open. Buttons flew as he shredded the garment, yanking it from her.

"No, let me go." She retreated into the fantasy, putting her hands on her breasts, over the lacy black bra she wore. "Leave me alone. Indy will kill you."

Of course, they had a safe word set, but there would probably be no reason to use it. Marc wasn't the kind of guy to take things too far.

He forced her hands away, holding both wrists in one hand as he yanked the flimsy lace from her breasts. His grip was firm, yet gentle. His fingers fondled her nipple as he brought his face to the side of her head, then ran his tongue up her neck to her ear. "He'll never find us here," he whispered. His breath was hot against her skin.

Candy had been with men who played rough. Marc was nothing like them. Still, he was playing his part, and trying hard to be the villain she needed. He just wasn't the kind of guy who would ever use force on a woman. It was time for drastic measures.

She pushed him back then swung her arm. As her palm connected with his cheek, a resounding smack reverberated in the small room. The slap sent Marc reeling. She hadn't meant to hit him that hard. Had she gone too far? Would *he* use the safe word?

Marc's eyes blazed with passion. "You'll pay for that."

No, there was an unguarded smile that creased the edge of his lips. He grabbed her wrist and dragged her toward the bed. Shackles hung from all four bedposts.

"No." She struggled, but not too hard, afraid he'd relent. "I'll scream."

"Scream all you like. No one will hear you here." He threw her on the bed and forced her right wrist into one of the cuffs, locking it tight. Using both hands on her left arm he pulled her across the bed and forced that shackle into place as well.

"Now you're not going anywhere." He began unbuttoning his shirt, backing away as Candy kicked at him.

Kneeling down, he sidled up toward the top of the bed, bending to run his tongue once again along her cheekbone as he fondled her bare breasts. "Soon you will learn to appreciate my attentions."

Oh, he was good. The slap must have awakened the true thespian within him. A chill ran through her core. Even deep down she was starting to believe, which is just what she wanted—what she needed.

Marc stood and brought his hands to the waistband of her skirt. With a fluid motion he whisked the garment down her legs, despite her kicking and wiggling. Grabbing each ankle, he discarded her shoes and stockings, then locked both feet in the lower bedpost shackles.

Spread eagle and defenseless, clad only in lacy, black bikini briefs, she struggled against her restraints. His hand crept up the inside of her leg, cupping her crotch. "Did you wear these just for me? They're very sexy." She felt his fingers pressing against her most intimate parts through the thin, silky fabric.

"But, of course, they have to go." He grabbed and pulled, ripping the skimpy panties from her body.

He backed away and turned, discarding the rest of his own clothing. When he turned back toward her, he held his cock in his hand. "You want this, don't you?"

Long, thick, and erect, the sight of Marc's cock caused a flow of passion in the deepest reaches of her core. Her mouth drooled at the thought of him taking her.

But that wasn't what she wanted tonight.

Someday, Marc...maybe...

Tonight, she needed Alan. He understood the deep, dark hole in her soul she was trying to fill.

Right from the start, so many men had taken from her. Alan knew her well enough to give back, and at least create the illusion that he cared. Tonight, she needed that. She needed her hero. Someone to rescue her from all those uncaring men. It was time to move the scenario along.

She tried to put a note of defiance in her tone. Steeling her visage, she stared daggers at Marc. "You'll never get away with this."

Come on Marc, give me evil.

"Baby, I already have." His sneer was perfect. Her body reacted with a molten flow.

Reaching down he palmed both her breasts, then gave each of the erect nipples a firm but gentle twist. "These are mine."

Candy thrashed back and forth, pulling the chains taught—fighting his grasp, as well as her body's ready acceptance of it.

Marc reached down, gliding his hand over her mound, then jammed two fingers into her hot, damp folds. "This is mine."

She wiggled again, resisting the temptation to push down and drive his fingers deeper into her.

"Bastard! Leave me alone." She felt her channel gushing warm liquid around Marc's probing fingers. The turn-on was incredible.

Marc climbed on the bed, kneeling between her legs, nudging them wider apart. He ran his hand along his shaft and shot her a sinister look. "I've been waiting for this a long time."

That was the verbal queue Alan would be waiting for. Her hero was about to arrive.

Marc positioned himself between her legs. The head of his cock nudged her folds as he prepared to enter her.

Then the door crashed open.

"Get away from her you bastard." Alan's husky voice filled the room and warmed her heart.

Yes!

The bed had been positioned to give her the perfect view. Alan stood silhouetted in the doorway. Khaki pants and shirt, battered leather jacket, brown fedora, and high leather boots. The bullwhip, borrowed from Room 7, hung on the left side of his belt. His right hand was pulling the paintball gun from the holster at his hip.

He was Indiana Jones. The stance, the look, and the gleam in his eyes all brought life to the fantasy Candy had so been craving.

Steel slid against leather, as Alan pulled the pistol and pointed it at Marc's chest. "I said, get away from her."

"Indy!" Candy's voice quivered as lightning shot through her core. Her hero had arrived.

"No! She's mine!" Marc managed to put desperation in his tone as he lunged forward. She felt the tip of his cock nudging her folds, seeking penetration.

Pop! Pop!

The two shots rang out and rivers of red ran down Marc's chest. He did a convincing job of having his eyes glaze before slumping over the side of the bed. Candy heard his body hit the floor with a dull thump.

But her eyes were on Alan. He strode heroically around the bed, coming to her side. "I'll have you out of those chains in no time."

"No Indy, I can't wait." The quiver and drama in her voice must have sounded comical, but she was truly out of control. She needed Alan so bad. "Take me like this. Take me now!"

The passionate gleam in Alan's eye was matched by the huge bulge in his pants.

Alan stripped off his jacket and shirt, then hung the fedora on the bedpost. He bent over her and ran a hand down the side of her face. "You're safe now. I'm never going to let anything happen to you ever again."

He brought his lips to hers. Strong, and sensual, his kiss took her to new heights. Her hero loved her, protected her, desired her.

She returned the kiss with full passion, probing with her tongue, wanting to consume him.

"Mmmm" The rumble came from deep in his throat. His lips and tongue continued to work their magic on her while he shed the rest of his clothing. She heard the gun belt hit the floor, followed by the soft swish of his pants zipper. The expanse of muscular, hot skin was a blur as he climbed onto the bed, his lips never leaving hers. The intensity of the kiss only deepened as he settled naked beside her.

She could feel the immensity of his cock against her leg. Johnson's *Johnson* was legendary in the Points Club. When fully erect, Alan had to be a full eleven inches of thick, glorious male member. Tonight, it would all be hers. As his fingers stroked her inner thigh, her channel slickened even more in anticipation.

"I want all of you," he said, breaking the kiss, then trailing butterfly flicks down the side of her neck, working his way toward her breast.

"Yes." She gasped as his lips found her ready nipple. His mouth locked onto the peak, sucking lightly on the tightly pebbled nub and flicking it with his tongue. Below, his fingers slipped into her, caressing and probing. Helpless in the shackles she squirmed beneath him, accepting his passionate strokes and surrendering completely to his ministrations.

Alan sucked hard, then released her breast, trailing kisses toward her navel. Kissing and licking, he laved her belly then continued lower still, readjusting to place one knee on each side of her head. Above her, thick, long, and hard, Alan's legendary cock hung erect and pulsing against her lips. Greedily Candy sucked the head into her mouth, licking gently and drinking in the droplet of semen that seeped from the tip.

"Ohhh." Alan groaned as she circled her tongue around and around. "You do know how to reward your rescuer."

Chapter 5

With Candy's mouth on his cock, Alan had all he could do to concentrate on his role. It wouldn't do for Indiana Jones to come too quickly, but what she was doing with her tongue was pure incredible torture.

Motion in his peripheral vision caught his attention. Marc Stevens was making good his escape from the room, crawling naked on all fours and quietly closing the door.

Alan was thankful for the diversion, as his balls had already started to tighten under Candy's assault. Marc's distraction gave him a chance to bear down and hold off his explosion. He wanted to give Candy the full measure for her points, but the woman was so hot—so sexy.

And God, did she know what to do with her tongue and lips. A cock wasn't safe anywhere in her proximity. Candy had elevated fellatio to a fine art form. There were men in the club who would ejaculate just thinking about what she'd done to them months earlier.

Well, Alan could give as well as he received. Diving down into the moistness between her legs, he dragged his tongue over her clit and along her folds, lapping at the juicy lubrication her body exuded. The aroma of lilac and pure woman filled his senses—a muskiness so intoxicating he was overwhelmed.

Wrapping his arms around and under her legs, he used his fingers to spread her folds and drove his tongue into her depths. Two could play at the oral sex game.

***

Helpless in the shackles, Candy writhed under Alan's assault. The scratchy hair of his five o'clock shadow dragged across her sensitive clitoris, stimulating nerve endings that shot sensations throughout her core. His tongue delved so deeply inside her, she clenched at each touch, each lick.

God in heaven! She couldn't concentrate. She'd taken his cock as deeply as she could, yet there was so much of him. She could only suck and lick and try to hold on to the shreds of her sanity.

Her passion crested and she had to release his cock to catch her breath before crying out in ecstasy. Waves of erotic fervor rolled over her, and she quivered under his manipulations. She barely felt the shackles release around her ankles as she rode the waves of orgasm.

She came back to herself and realized he'd shifted back to the top and released her wrists as well. Gently he took her in his arms and kissed her forehead, then her cheek.

"I love you pumpkin." The words were soft, spoken under his breath. How she wished Alan truly meant them. He sold them with a passion that surprised her, yet she knew his words were false.

No man could love her. She was a broken woman, and certainly undeserving of someone like this. The darkness within her was more than anyone would want to bear. Points Club could only give her the illusion, the fantasy. But that was enough. It had to be.

Her hands now free, she reached down and wrapped fingers around Alan's glorious cock. Hard and pulsing in her hand, she knew he was close to release. And she wanted to give him that—give him everything.

"You always give so much." She wasn't sure if she was still acting or not. He did always give so much. "Take me. Take all that you want, all that you need."

Alan knew he would never get what he really needed. He'd take what she offered and give back all he could, but his darkness would extinguish the bright light that was Candy Kane.

The feel of her lithe fingers on his cock was heavenly. Alan hugged her close, cradling her soft body against him. With her in his arms he could pretend he was lovable, and the darkness within him receded for the moment.

Her body was perfect, alluring, and sexy as hell, but it was her essence that truly attracted Alan. The woman beneath those smooth curves was devilish yet childlike, and so full of life. In a group like Points Club, those qualities shone like the sun, breaking from the clouds after a stormy night.

He'd often maneuvered to be the one to fill her fantasies, because she so perfectly filled his. He pulled her close, softly kissing her ruby lips. He felt her body respond and he intensified the kiss, probing with his tongue.

Sliding his hand up her side he cupped her perfect breast, enjoying the pliant buoyancy. The nipple, standing erect, beckoned him, and he brushed his thumb over it, feeling the quiver in her body that the action induced.

He wrapped his arm back around her then, drawing her close and enjoying the feel of her breasts pressed against his chest. All the while she continued to stroke his cock, keeping him on the edge of orgasm.

He fought it, wanting the moment to last, but knowing all too soon he would need to sheath himself in her warmth and let his animal instincts loose.

He broke off the kiss. "The things you do to me."

She smiled up at him, her eyes bright with passion. "And you, my hero. The things you do to me."

He chuckled, throwing himself back into his role. "They are nothing compared to the things I am *about* to do to you."

He moved his hand down to cup her buttocks, pulling her closer to him. The heat of her skin on his was excruciatingly sensual.

"Indeed sir? Then you should get on with it."

She disengaged and rolled to her back, spreading her legs suggestively. Alan felt his cock pulse in need. The need to be inside her was all-powerful.

Alan shifted his position to between those incredible long legs and guided his cock to the entrance of her channel, dragging the spongy head along her damp folds, teasing her.

Candy was more than ready. Damp with lubrication, he easily glided into her, though he did it slowly to allow her to adjust to his girth. The last thing he ever wanted to do, would be to hurt her, or cause her discomfort, in a rush for his own release. He'd been endowed with a big cock, but with great girth came great responsibility.

As if reading his thoughts, Candy groaned and responded. "Damn it Alan, slam that thing into me. You know I can take it, and right now, damn it, I need it...bad!"

Alan smiled, sheathing his cock balls deep. "Your wish, fair maiden, is my command."

This was, after all, her fantasy.

***

"Maiden my ass," Candy remarked as Alan withdrew and slammed into her once again. She

140

hadn't been a maiden in over fifteen years, her virginity stolen one dark, terrible night.

For years she'd thought she'd brought it on herself...deserved what she'd gotten. Sex was all she was good for, after all. So, she became very good at it.

Points Club had been the perfect place to practice her craft. Every man wanted her. Every woman wanted to be her. But while outwardly she'd kept up the façade of the passionate, devil-may-care sex kitten, inside the frightened little girl still wanted the fantasy, the hero who would love her for her. And save her from...herself.

At first, she'd hated all men, but through the club, she'd met some good men...gentle men. Guys like Alan, who could at least give her the illusion and keep alive the fantasy. Guys who could fill the desperate, needy hole in her soul.

Alan stroked a third time, quickening his pace and filling her so completely she found herself clenching around his shaft.

"Oh God, I love it when you do that." Alan's face was awash with passion. His eyes blazed and he pistoned in and out. His shaft, so thick, so long, it hit every erogenous spot Candy possessed.

Explosions danced throughout her core and the passionate waves rose within her. She could tell he was close when his massive organ grew even bigger within her. Harder and deeper he delved her depths and the feeling of ecstasy rose to devour her.

Alan's release came hard and heavy, and Candy could feel the warm gush of each strong jet. The passion drove her over the cliff of her own orgasm, and her world spun. Waves of pure pleasure washed over her. Control shattered and she was swept away in a flood of emotion.

Alan collapsed on her, cocooning her in his warmth. It wasn't crushing. She felt protected and cherished. His arms drew her in, and he held her gently. His lips trailed warm, wet kisses on her neck.

He rolled, bringing her with him and settling her on top of him.

"Kiss me, Pumpkin." His smile was infectious, and she lowered her lips to his.

When had he picked out a pet name for her? Candy tried to recall if he'd ever called her *Pumpkin* before. He knew that part of her fantasy was always the cuddling afterward. He was probably just adding something personal to the fantasy. That was so like him.

She ran fingers through his shaggy, damp hair and feasted on his lips. God, he felt so good. Muscles rippled under his hot skin. She could have lain here caressing him forever.

But their time was up, the fantasy was over. It was time to return to the real world. She pressed hard, one last time, then broke off the kiss.

"Thanks Alan, that was perfect." She rose from the bed and stood just watching Alan roll to the other side of the bed and rise.

"It was fun," he said throwing her a smile. "Any time you want a repeat, give me a call."

How about every night from now until forever?

For once her mind didn't allow her to let go. If only...

Her prop clothes were in tatters. Her street clothes were hanging in the anteroom. She should go and get dressed, but she wasn't ready to leave yet. Once she went through that door, she'd have to face the real world again.

Alan was slipping back into the Indiana Jones gear. He looked so good. "Do you want me to send this stuff back to you?"

She forced a smile and shook her head. "Keep it, if you would. You can count on me calling you again."

But she wasn't sure she'd call. Somehow this was hurting far worse than it should have. Her hero was leaving her.

After he finished dressing, Alan stooped to pick up the whip and the gun. "I'll return these to their proper places on my way out."

She kept her smile in place, but inside she was crumbling. This wasn't at all how she'd thought it would go tonight. She'd hit to close to what she really wanted...what she could never have.

Chapter 7

Alan stood watching Candy in all her naked splendor. He was loath to leave and considered offering her points to continue their time together. But what would they do? Points were only for sex, and it would be a while before he was ready again.

She probably had a party or something planned anyway. Someone like Candy would be in demand. If he tried to monopolize her time, she'd know how he felt about her. She'd probably laugh. What he was feeling wasn't allowed in Points Club.

Her effervescent smile lit the room, and he gave her lush body one last good look before preparing to leave. Suddenly her face fell.

It was just for a moment, before she turned, crossed her arms and faced the corner of the room, but he saw it...the look in her eyes. With sudden clarity he saw it all. He knew that look; he'd seen it in the mirror.

***

Candy felt the chill in her gut as the gloom and darkness rose. It wasn't supposed to be like this. It was supposed to be fun—fulfilling. But all she felt was emptiness. She kept the smile in place as long as she could, then turned quickly away from Alan so he wouldn't see her sorrow. Tears welled in her eyes.

Leave, Allen. Just leave now.

She heard a gentle swish, and the end of the bullwhip suddenly wrapped itself around her middle. She turned back toward Alan, cocking her head in question.

He pulled on the bullwhip, dragging her to him across the room.

"Would you like to go get a cup of coffee with me?"

Chapter 8

This was a mistake. Points Club members were not supposed to talk about what happened in the club. Candy sat across from Alan, in one of the back booths of an all-night diner just down the street from the club.

It had taken everything Candy had to rein in her emotions. Coffee with Alan sounded so good, a continuation of their time together. It was wrong, but it felt so right she couldn't help herself.

"You know," Alan said. "I've known you for almost ten years now, but I don't know anything about you. What's your favorite pie?"

The question came out of nowhere. What was Alan up to?

"Lemon meringue, why?"

He just smiled and motioned the waitress over. "Two coffee and a piece of lemon meringue pie...with two forks."

The waitress left to fill the order, and Alan sat back in his seat, just looking at her.

"Okay, Alan, spill. What's going on?"

He took a deep breath, but didn't speak right away, as if considering his words.

"Would you like to go out for dinner tomorrow night? Maybe take in a movie?"

God, it sounded like he was asking her out on a date.

"What is this, some new fantasy you're working on?"

Alan reached across the table, taking her hand. The warmth of the contact caused her to look up into Alan's eyes. What she saw there, caused her stomach to do a flip.

"No, Pumpkin," he said simply. "This is something real."

If you liked this book, please consider giving it a review on Amazon at:
https://books2read.com/u/3RJplL

I also post regular short erotic stories on **Medium.com**:
https://medium.com/@marcstevens_87662
(Not a medium member? You can sign up with my link to support my writing. Go here:
https://medium.com/@marcstevens_87662/membership)

I also blog about my books, sales, and giveaways at:
https://marcstevenserotica.wordpress.com/

Bio: Marc Stevens' Erotic Adventures.

I'm not real. I'm a pen name – a stock image. I write sexy stuff, sometimes dark, sometimes humorous, sometimes thought provoking. I write what I want. Like it or don't, I really don't care.

Marc Stevens.

Points Club Series

A spicy sex club with lots of secrets.

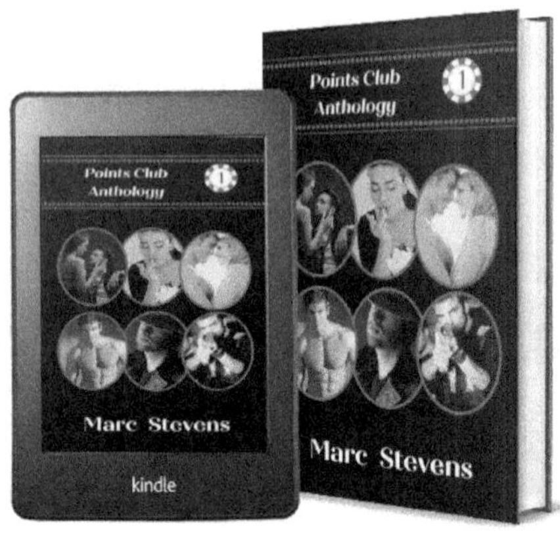

Other books by Marc Stevens